Harlequin Romance is excited to present this
timeless duet from award-winning author
Lucy Gordon

When true love is eternal...

A Winter Proposal

Meet Pippa Jensen.
Her grandparents proved to her that true love
does exist, so Pippa is unwilling to settle for
anything less than the perfect man.

Can brooding stockbroker Roscoe Havering
be *the one* for her?

His Diamond Bride

Meet Pippa's grandparents.
Dee and Mark Sellon's love spans
sixty years, but the course of true love
never runs smooth....

This is their heart-wrenching,
uplifting and timeless story.

Dear Reader,

Given the way my last heroine, Pippa, was influenced by Dee, her grandmother, there was no way I could write Pippa's story without also writing Dee's. She came from another age when men and women saw each other in more traditional roles, and the obstacles to love were different, obstacles like the turmoil caused by war.

Unlike Pippa, Dee was not spectacularly beautiful. Pleasant but unremarkable, she chose a useful life as a nurse. The beauty of the family was her sister Sylvia and, when she brought home the handsome Mark Sellon, Dee was content to admire him from a distance.

Then he became a pilot, flying daring missions and being hailed as a hero. To Dee this glamorous man seemed more out of her reach than ever. How could he ever love her? And how could she ever believe in his love?

Mark, lost in confusion, struggling to recover from terrible experiences, could make his way only slowly toward the love of his life, but when he saw his destiny, lit up and beckoning, he pursued it with determined purpose.

The road to each other was complicated and troublesome, with pain and despair as well as joy. At the end of it lay their sixtieth wedding anniversary, celebrated publicly with diamonds, but privately with a contentment of heart that they would once have thought impossible.

It was the triumphant achievement of that joy that gave Dee a new mission in life, to reach out to her beloved granddaughter, helping Pippa find the way to her own happiness.

Warmest wishes,

Lucy Gordon

LUCY GORDON
His Diamond Bride

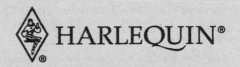

TORONTO • NEW YORK • LONDON
AMSTERDAM • PARIS • SYDNEY • HAMBURG
STOCKHOLM • ATHENS • TOKYO • MILAN • MADRID
PRAGUE • WARSAW • BUDAPEST • AUCKLAND

Recycling programs
for this product may
not exist in your area.

ISBN-13: 978-0-373-17707-3

HIS DIAMOND BRIDE

First North American Publication 2011

Lucy Gordon cut her writing teeth on magazine journalism, interviewing many of the world's most interesting men, including Warren Beatty, Charlton Heston and Roger Moore. She also camped out with lions in Africa, and had many other unusual experiences, which have often provided the background for her books. Several years ago, while staying in Venice, she met a Venetian who proposed in two days. They have been married ever since. Naturally this has affected her writing, where romantic Italian men tend to feature strongly.

Two of her books have won the Romance Writers of America RITA® Award. You can visit her website at www.lucy-gordon.com.

CHAPTER ONE

5th August 2003

'HE MUST have been the most handsome man who ever lived,' Pippa sighed, her eyes fixed on the framed photograph in her hands. 'Look at those film star features and the way he's half smiling, as though at a private joke.'

'That's what used to drive the other girls wild,' Lilian said. 'Mum said he could charm the birds off the trees, and always keep them wondering.'

She was fifty-eight, with grey hair and a vivid face. She smiled when she spoke of her parents.

The photograph had been taken sixty-three years earlier. It showed a fine-looking young man, splendid in airman's uniform, his head slightly cocked, his features alive with sardonic humour. It bore only a faint resemblance to the old man that he was now, but the glint in his eyes had survived.

He was crouching on the wing of an aeroplane, one arm resting on a raised knee, his face turned to the camera, yet with a mysterious air of gazing into the future, as though he could see what was coming and was eager to meet it. Everything in the picture was redolent of life and masculine attraction.

'He may have been a hero back then, but I'll bet he was a devil, too,' Pippa said gleefully.

She was just twenty-one and beautiful. Her mother was immensely proud of her but she didn't let that show too often.

'Too attractive for her own good,' was her favourite expression to conceal her pride.

'Yes, I've heard he was a devil, among many other things,' she agreed, looking back at the picture of Flight Lieutenant Mark Sellon. 'By the way, the local TV station has been in touch. They want to do a piece—hero and wife celebrate sixty years of marriage. And the local paper. They're both sending someone to the party this afternoon to get some pictures and a few words about all the fantastic things he did in the war.'

'Grandpa won't like that,' Pippa observed. 'He hates going back over that time. Have you ever realised how little we actually know about it? He always avoids the subject. "Ask Gran", he says. But she doesn't tell much either.'

'I wish they'd let me throw the party in my house,' Lilian said. 'It's bigger and we could have got more people in.' She looked around disparagingly at the modest little property that stood at the far end of Crimea Street on the outskirts of London.

'It's where it all began,' Pippa reminded her. 'They met when he came to stay here with the family the last Christmas before the war, and all over the house there are places that remind her of him as he was then.'

'I suppose now you know them better than any of us,' Lilian said.

Pippa was her youngest child, several years younger than her siblings, arriving when the others were all at school and Lilian had resumed her career as a midwife. Lilian's mother had come to the rescue, announcing that, as they lived only three streets apart, she could take on most of the baby's care. The result was that Pippa had always been close to her grandparents, regarding them almost as extra parents.

She was spirited, even rebellious and in her teens this had led to difficulties with Lilian, resulting in her taking shelter in Crimea Street. The trouble had been smoothed out. Mother and daughter were friends again, but Pippa now lived with her grandparents, keeping a protective eye on them as they grew old and frail.

On the surface it was a perfect arrangement, yet Pippa was a worry to all who loved her. With her brains and beauty she should have been doing something more demanding than a dead-end job, and her social life should have consisted of more than staying at home almost every evening.

All the fault of Jack Sothern, Lilian thought bitterly. He'd seemed like a decent fellow, and everyone had been happy when he became engaged to Pippa. But he'd broken it off ruthlessly just a few weeks before the planned Christmas wedding, leaving Pippa devastated.

That had been nine months ago. Pippa had seemed to recover, but the life had gone out of her, as though she was emotionally flattened. She still smiled and laughed with a charm that won everyone over, but behind her eyes there was a blankness that never changed.

The doorbell rang and Lilian went to answer it. After that she was kept busy letting in guests until the house was overflowing. Pippa welcomed everyone with a finger over her lips.

'They're upstairs lying down,' she whispered. 'I want them to rest until the last minute. Tonight's going to be very tiring for them.'

Lilian's brother Terry appeared. He was in his fifties, heavily built with greying hair and bullish features that radiated good nature. With him was his wife Celia, two children and three grandchildren. Hard on his heels came Irene, his first wife, now remarried, also with a herd of youngsters.

'I can't even keep track of them,' Pippa confided to her Uncle Terry. 'Are we related to them all?'

'We're definitely related to that one,' Terry observed, indicating a boy of fourteen who seemed possessed by an imp of mischief. 'Mum says he's exactly like Dad was years ago: into everything, driving everyone mad, then winning them over with that smile. But he's bright; always top of the class, apparently.'

'He didn't get that from Grandpa,' Pippa remarked. 'He was bottom of the class, according to him. He says there was always something more interesting to do than read dreary books, and there still is.'

Terry laughed appreciatively. 'That sounds like Dad. His idea of serious reading is a magazine with pretty girls. I hope he doesn't let Mum see them.'

Pippa chuckled. 'She's not bothered. She buys them for him.'

Terry nodded. 'That sounds just like her.'

'Have you got all the pictures out?' Terry asked.

'Yes, they're in here.' She led the way to a room at the back, decorated for the party, hung with paper chains and flowers and full of photographs. Some were family groups, but most were individual shots.

There was Lilian on her twenty-first birthday. There was Terry dressed for mountain climbing, which was his passion.

'What about Gran's parents?' Pippa asked, pointing to a picture of a middle-aged couple dressed in the clothes of the thirties. 'Should I have put them a bit further forward?'

'Yes, I think so. It would please her.' He reached for another picture, showing a beautiful young woman with a ripe, curvy figure. 'And this one, of her sister Sylvia.'

'Ah, Great Aunt Sylvia,' Pippa said. 'I often wish I'd known her, she sounds so interesting. Wasn't she the one who—?'

'Yes, she was. It was an earth-shattering scandal at the time, but these days nobody would think anything of it. Times have changed. Put her where she can be seen. Mum was very fond of her.' He looked around for a moment before adding, 'There's one missing. Polly should be there, too.'

'Should she? I did wonder, and I've got some pictures of

her, just in case. But she was only a year old when she died. She barely existed.'

'Don't let them hear you say that,' Terry said in alarm. 'Dad absolutely adored my baby sister. It's nearly fifty years since she died, but she's still part of the family, and if you leave her out he'll be upset.'

'Yes, of course. Here she is,' Pippa agreed.

She produced two photographs, one a portrait of a baby girl, beaming at the camera, the other showing the same child in her father's arms. Their eyes were locked, each totally entranced by the other.

'He was a terrific dad,' Terry said, studying the picture. 'But I don't think he ever looked at any of the rest of us quite like that. It was just something Polly had, maybe because she was the image of Mum...I don't know...'

'You think it had something to do with the way he felt about Gran?'

'I'm not sure, but when Polly died, I think he'd have gone crazy if it hadn't been for her.'

'When he walks into a room he always looks to see if she's there,' Pippa reflected. 'If she isn't, he keeps looking at the door, waiting for her to arrive. And when she does arrive, he seems to settle down.'

The bell rang and she went to let in the reporter from the local TV station, a young woman called Stacey, and the photographer, who prowled around looking for angles.

'I just can't get over anyone being married sixty years,' Stacey said, awed.

'It was different in their day,' Pippa said. 'People married for life. And I think Grandpa was courting her for a long time so he wasn't going to let her go easily.'

'Long courtship,' Stacey muttered, making notes. 'Good, that gives me something to go on.'

At last everyone was there: Mark and Dee's children and

grandchildren, cousins, in-laws, a representative from the local hospital where Dee had once worked.

'Quiet everybody! They're coming.'

The photographer got into position at the bottom of the stairs, ready to capture the stars of the evening as they appeared above: Mr and Mrs Sellon, Mark and Deirdre, known to everyone as Dee. They were in their eighties, white-haired, thin and frail-looking, but holding themselves erect, with smiling eyes.

They descended the stairs arm in arm, seeming to support each other equally, until the moment Dee stumbled and clung to her husband for safety.

'Careful, my love,' he said, guiding her to a chair. 'What happened?'

'Nothing; I tripped on the carpet.'

'Are you sure you're all right? You'd better have a cup of tea.'

'Tea?' she said in mock outrage. 'Today? I want a good strong sherry.'

He hurried to get her a glass and Lilian regarded them with delight.

'Look how he dances attendance on her,' she sighed. 'After all these years. So many husbands become indifferent.'

'I've never known Grandpa indifferent,' Pippa said. 'In fact, he sometimes smothers Gran with his concern. He's so scared that she'll go first.'

'You know the saying. There's always one who loves and one who lets themselves be loved,' Lilian reminded her. 'No prizes for guessing which is which with those two.'

Even as she spoke, Dee's voice rose, full of affectionate laughter. 'Darling, I'm all right. Will you stop fussing?'

Everyone heard that, but only she heard his murmured response. 'No, I won't, and you know that I won't. You've been telling me for years to stop fussing over you and I've never listened yet, so why don't you just give up?'

'I never give up where you're concerned,' she whispered back. 'You should know that by now.'

'I do know it. I rely on it.'

He touched her face gently. It had never been a beautiful face, but it had always been rich in warmth and generosity, qualities that the years had left untouched. Watching them, the family knew that what he'd first seen in her years ago, he saw there still.

The elderly couple were shown into the main party room and went around the collection of family photographs, pausing occasionally to murmur to each other, words that nobody else could hear. When it came to baby Polly, Gran lifted the picture and they looked at it together before they met each other's gaze and nodded.

'I swear there were tears in Grandpa's eyes,' Pippa murmured afterwards.

At last they were seated together on the sofa while family members approached them, hugging and murmuring words of congratulation. Champagne was poured and glasses were raised in toasts. Speeches were made. Everyone wanted to have their say.

Then Stacey got to work, talking to the camera.

'…one of the last of a dying breed…heroes of World War Two, who gave their all for their country…night after night, climbing into their Spitfires, taking off into the darkness, not knowing if they would return to their loved ones…how proud we are that one of them is still among us…'

'Is she going to witter on like that for ever?' Mark growled under his breath.

'Hush,' Dee murmured. 'Let your family take pride in you.'

'My family know nothing about it,' he insisted.

'How can they? They weren't born then. Don't blame them for that.'

Out of sight, they squeezed each other's hands.

Now Stacey turned her attention on them. To her questions about the war Mark gave polite but uninformative replies, claiming to have forgotten the details. Finally she said, 'But I understand that yours is also a great romance. Mr Sellon, is it true that you courted your wife for years before you persuaded her to marry you?'

'Oh, yes,' Mark said. 'She wasn't won easily. I really had to work hard to impress her.'

Everyone smiled at this. Only the most perceptive noticed the look of surprise on Dee's face.

'But how romantic!' Stacey exclaimed. 'The lover who yearns hopelessly from afar. Mrs Sellon, why did you make him wait so long?'

'I'm not sure now. We weren't the same people back then.'

'Would you do it any differently now?'

Dee's lips twitched. 'Oh, yes,' she said. 'I'd make him wait *much* longer.'

The newspaper journalist followed, with similar questions, but he had his eye on the photograph of Flight Lieutenant Sellon that the family had studied earlier.

'This is a fantastic picture,' he said. 'I'd like to use it in the paper. I'll need to borrow it—'

'No,' Dee said at once. 'I'm sorry; you can't take it away.'

'Just for a few hours. I'll take care—'

'I'm sure you will, but I can't take the risk. I'm sorry.' Her manner was polite but very firm as she removed the picture from his hand. 'This is mine.'

The young man looked round for help, but none of the family would yield. They knew Gran when she spoke like that.

The evening moved gently on to its conclusion, everyone feeling that it had been a triumphant success. In the spotlight, Mark and Dee seemed to be enjoying themselves but, as he slipped his arm about her waist, he murmured, 'When will they go?'

'Soon,' she promised.

They smiled at one another and the camera clicked. The picture appeared in the local paper the next day. Neither of them noticed it being taken.

At last it was all over. The guests departed, and Lilian accompanied her parents up to their room.

'How is Pippa coping?' Dee wanted to know. 'I worried about her this evening. A wedding anniversary. How that must have hurt her! If her wedding had gone ahead, it would have been her own first anniversary soon.'

'I know, but you'd never guess it, she seems so bright,' Lilian sighed. 'Oh, I could kill that man for what he did to her.'

Pippa's entry silenced the topic. Together, they helped the old people to bed, kissed them goodnight and retreated to the door.

'You're not too tired after all the goings-on?' Pippa asked.

'Tired?' Mark echoed. 'We're only just starting. We're going to get revved up, then swing from the chandeliers and indulge in some mad lust. You youngsters! You don't know how to enjoy life. Ow! No need to beat me up.'

Dee, who'd delivered the lightest tap on his shoulder, chuckled. 'Behave yourself!' she commanded.

'You see how she treats me,' Mark sighed. 'I expect you bully your menfolk too, and they wonder where you get it from. They should see what I put up with. Ow!'

As the two old people collapsed with laughter, Lilian drew her daughter away.

'Let's leave them to it. Honestly, they're like a couple of kids.'

'Perhaps that's their secret,' Pippa said.

'Yes,' Lilian said thoughtfully. 'They do seem to have a secret, don't they?'

They went downstairs to get on with the clearing up.

In the darkness, Mark and Dee listened to the fading footsteps.

'We're very lucky,' she mused, 'that our family takes such care of us.'

'True, but I hope they don't come back,' he admitted. 'Right now, I want to be alone with you. What are you giggling for?'

'I was remembering the first time you ever said that to me. I was so thrilled. Suddenly every dream I'd ever had was coming true.'

'But it wasn't, was it?' he reminded her. 'I was a dreadful character in those days. I can't think what you saw in me.'

'Well, if you don't know, I'm not going to tell you,' she teased. 'We had our troubles, but we reached home in the end. That's all that matters.'

'Yes, we reached home and shut the door against the world,' he mused. 'And, ever since then, we've kept each other safe. Sixty years you've put up with me! I can't imagine how!'

'Neither can I, so stop fishing for compliments. And, by the way, what game were you playing tonight?'

'Game? I don't know what you mean.'

'Don't play the innocent with me. All that talk about how you had to court me for years and work to impress me. You know that's not what happened.'

'Yes, it is.'

'It most certainly is not. Don't you remember—?'

He stopped her with a gentle finger over her mouth. 'Hush! I remember what I remember, and you remember what you remember, and maybe it's not the same thing, but does that matter?'

'No, I suppose not,' she said thoughtfully. 'I dare say we'll never know now which of us has remembered it right.'

'Both of us and neither of us,' he said.

She smiled. 'You're very wise tonight.'

'I'll swear that's the first time you've ever called me wise. Now, tell me, did you like your present?'

'I loved it, but you shouldn't have splashed out on diamonds.'

'*One* measly little diamond,' he corrected. 'I was determined you were going to have that on our diamond anniversary.' Then his voice rose in horror. '*Good grief; I almost forgot!* Your other present.'

'I've been wondering about that, ever since you told me this morning that the diamond was only the "official" present, and that you had something else for me that meant much more. You said you'd give it to me later, when the crowd had gone.'

'I forgot until now,' he groaned.

'Never mind, darling,' she said tenderly. 'People of our age become forgetful.'

'Our age?' he echoed, affronted. 'Are you suggesting that I'm old?'

'Of course not. You could be a hundred and you still wouldn't be old.'

'Thank you, my dear.'

She couldn't resist adding cheekily, 'But give me my present before you forget again.'

He gave her a look, then switched on the little light by the bed and fumbled in a drawer, producing a small object that he hid behind his back. 'Close your eyes and hold out your hands,' he ordered.

Smiling, she did so, until she felt the soft touch of fur in her palm, and opened her eyes to find a small teddy bear. She gave an excited squeal and rubbed him against her cheek. 'Now, that's a real present,' she said. '*Much* better than diamonds.'

There seemed little in the toy to explain her delight. Six inches tall, with beady eyes and nylon fur, he was like a thousand other cheap trinkets, but Dee was overwhelmed with joy.

'Do you remember the first one I gave you?' Mark asked fondly.

For answer, she reached under her pillow and produced another toy bear. Once, long ago, he might have been like the new one, but now all his fur had worn away, he was shabby and mended at the seams.

'He's still here,' Dee said, holding him up. 'I never let him get far away.'

'You talk as though he was alive and trying to escape.'

'He is alive, and he knows he can never escape me,' she said, looking at her husband with meaning. 'That night you said you'd given him to me so that I didn't forget you. I loved you so much that nothing in the world could have made me forget you, but you didn't know that.'

'I took too long to understand,' he agreed. 'So many things I didn't see until it was nearly too late.'

'But I always had my Mad Bruin,' she said, indicating the threadbare toy.

'Mad Bruin,' he said, taking the bear from her and holding him up to consider him. 'I remember when you called me that. You were so angry. You were an impressive woman when you got really mad. Still are.'

'You scared me, doing something so stupid,' she recalled. 'You were the real Mad Bruin. Mad as a hatter, always doing something no sensible man would have done.'

'And we both got told off,' he remembered, addressing the toy.

She held both of the tiny bears together. 'He'll enjoy having a companion. I'm glad you gave me this. It was a lovely thing to think of. I thought you'd forgotten all about Bruin.'

'No, I didn't forget, but I noticed that you keep him hidden away.'

'Nobody else would understand.'

'Nobody but us,' he agreed.

She slipped both toys under her pillow. Mark turned out the lamp and they settled down together in the darkness. She felt his arms go around her, while her head found its natural place on his shoulder.

'Bliss,' he mused. 'This is what I've been waiting for all evening. Everyone is kind to us, but they don't understand. They just never know.'

'No,' she murmured. 'Only we know, but only we *need* to know.'

'Goodnight, my darling.'

'Goodnight.'

After a moment she heard the change in his breathing that meant he was asleep. But she wasn't ready to sleep. The evening had revived sixty years of memories and now they seemed to be there, dancing in the darkness.

The old man beside her disappeared, leaving only the dazzling young hero of long ago. How stunned she'd been by her first experience of love, blissful if he smiled at her, despairing because she knew he could never he hers.

Slowly she raised herself on one elbow to look down on him in gentle adoration. He awoke at once.

'What is it?' he asked quickly. 'Is something wrong?'

'Nothing,' she reassured him, settling back into his arms. 'Go to sleep.'

Content, he closed his eyes again. But she did not sleep. She lay looking into the distance, remembering

CHAPTER TWO

December 1938

'ANY sign of them yet?' Helen Parsons' voice sang out from the kitchen.

Dee, her seventeen-year-old daughter, paused from studying a box of Christmas decorations and went to the window. The narrow London street outside seemed empty, but the darkness made it hard to see far so she slipped out of the front door and down the small garden to the gate.

'Not a sign,' she said, returning to the house and hurriedly closing the door.

Her mother appeared, frowning. 'Have you been out without a coat, in this weather?'

'Just for a moment.'

'You'll catch your death of cold. You're a nurse; you should have more sense.'

Dee chuckled good-humouredly. 'It's a bit soon to call me a nurse. I've barely started my training.'

'Don't tell your father that. He's dead proud of you. He tells everyone that his daughter became a nurse because she's the bright one of the family.'

The bright one, Dee thought wryly. Her older sister, Sylvia, was the beautiful one, and she was the bright one.

'Now, don't start that again,' her mother said, reading her face without trouble.

'It's just that sometimes I'd like to be gorgeous, like Sylvia,' Dee said wistfully.

'Nonsense, you're pretty enough.' She bustled back to the kitchen, leaving Dee to gaze into the mirror.

She had pleasant, regular features under short brown hair, with dark brown expressive eyes. Pretty enough. That was about the best anyone could say and, if it hadn't been for Sylvia, Dee might have been content with it. But when she compared Sylvia's luscious features with her own, which were pleasant but not spectacular, she knew she could never be content.

Her figure was slender, almost too much so, which would have pleased many girls. But they didn't have the constant comparison with Sylvia's ripe curves. Dee didn't appreciate her own shape—with all the yearning of seventeen, she wanted Sylvia's.

She wanted to be beautiful, she wanted boyfriends trailing after her, and a throaty, seductive voice. Instead, she was 'the bright one' and 'pretty enough'. As though that was any comfort. Honestly! Older people just didn't understand.

'I wonder what this one's like,' her mother said, returning with a duster that she put into Dee's hand.

No need to ask who 'this one' was. Yet another of Sylvia's conquests. There were so many.

'She'll get a bad name, having a new young man every week,' Helen observed.

'But at least she's got some choice,' Dee observed wistfully. 'Not like being stuck with Charlie Whatsit down the road, or the man who comes round with the pies every week.'

'I don't want this family being talked about,' Helen said firmly. 'It isn't nice. Anyway, what about all those doctors you meet at the hospital?'

'They don't look at student nurses. We're the lowest of the low.'

'The patients, then. You wait, you'll meet a millionaire. He'll take one look at you and fall madly in love.'

They laughed together and Dee said, 'Mum, you've been reading those romantic novels again. That's just dreaming. Real life isn't like that—unless you're Sylvia, of course. I wish she'd hurry up and get here. I'm longing to see her latest.'

Sylvia worked in an elegant dress shop on the far side of London. As Christmas neared, business was booming and her hours were longer. Today she was arriving home late, along with her new young man.

Mark Sellon was a mechanic, newly out of work because his employer had lost all his money. Sylvia was bringing him home for Christmas in the hope that her father could offer him a job in the tiny garage he owned beside the house in Crimea Street. In that shabby corner of London, Joe Parsons counted as a prosperous man.

'Of course, he might simply be a good mechanic, and she's bringing him for Dad's sake,' Dee mused.

'Then why would she want us to invite him to stay the night? By the way, have you finished putting the spare bed into her room?'

'Yes, but—'

'You'll sleep there with Sylvia. And make sure you stay with her as much as possible. I don't want any hanky-panky in this house.'

'You mean—?'

'Yes, that's exactly what I mean, so you see that Sylvia behaves herself. Thank goodness I don't have to worry about you!'

Dee knew better than to answer this. To say that she yearned to be a 'bad girl', in theory if not in practice, would bring motherly wrath down about her head and she had some urgent dusting to do.

In this she was helped by Billy, the family dog, an enormous mongrel who tackled everything with gusto. His contribution to the cleaning was to follow Dee everywhere, pouncing on the dusters and shaking them.

'Let go,' she told him, trying to sound stern and not succeeding. 'Billy, I shall get cross with you.'

His glance said he'd heard that before and knew better than to believe it.

'Stop it, you idiot!' she said through laughter, managing to rescue a duster. His response was to seize another and run off.

'You haven't got time for play,' Helen said, appearing. 'They'll be here soon.'

'Yes, Mum.'

She applied herself to the work, finished it as soon as possible, then said, 'I'm taking Billy for a walk. He needs exercise or he won't behave himself.'

'All right, but don't be too long.'

She pulled on a thick coat and slipped out of the door, with Billy on a lead. It was a beautiful clear night, stars and moon shining down with a dazzling intensity that revealed her surroundings sharply.

'Shame there's no snow,' she mused. 'Never mind. Still, a little time before Christmas Day... All right Billy, *I'm coming.*'

Down the street he hauled her, across the road into another long street and down a narrow path that went along a string of back gardens. Voices greeted her as she went, for she had lived here all her life and knew the neighbours.

Now Billy was on his way back, taking her for a walk rather than the other way round. As they reached Crimea Street, she heard a sound in the distance, quickly growing louder and louder until it was deafening.

Then she saw a motorbike turning the corner, coming towards her, driven by someone in a helmet and goggles that obscured his head. In the sidecar was another person, also

mysterious until it raised an arm to wave at her and Dee realised that it was Sylvia.

So the driver must be her young man. Dee stared in wonder.
She'd sometimes seen motorbikes being repaired in her father's
garage, but she knew nobody who actually owned one.

The bike stopped and the driver got off to help Sylvia out,
then remove her helmet. She clung to him, wide-eyed.

'Oh, goodness!' she gasped. 'That was—that was—'

'Are you all right?' Dee asked.

Sylvia's response was to release her companion and throw
her arms around Dee as if her legs were giving way beneath
her, so that Dee had to support her.

She glanced at the young man. He was removing his goggles and the first part of him she saw was a smiling mouth—
something she afterwards remembered all her life.

Then his whole face was revealed—handsome, lively, full
of pleasure.

'Sorry if I was a bit noisy,' he said ruefully. 'When I'm
going really fast the excitement tends to carry me away. I'm
afraid I've offended your neighbours.'

The words sounded contrite but there was nothing contrite
about him. He'd enjoyed himself to the full and was fizzing
with delight. All around them curtains were being pulled
back, shocked faces appearing at windows. He greeted them
with a cheeky wave before turning back to Sylvia.

'I'm sorry,' he repeated. 'I didn't mean to scare you.'

'I never dreamed you'd go so fast,' Sylvia gasped. 'It was—
oh, goodness!'

She took a deep breath and remembered her manners.
'Mark, this is my sister, Dee. Dee, this is Mark.'

Now Dee could look at him properly and her head swam.
He was too good-looking to be true. It didn't happen outside
the cinema. She held out her hand and from a distance heard
him saying that Sylvia had told him all about her.

'Nothing bad, I hope,' she said mechanically and immediately cursed herself for talking nonsense. But it was as much as she could do to talk at all.

A moment ago she'd been content with life trundling along in the same old way. Now it was as though a thunderbolt had struck her.

'Let's get inside,' Sylvia said. 'It's freezing out here.'

Joe and Helen had come to the door to see what all the commotion was about. The sight of Mark wheeling his motorbike brought Joe hurrying down the path of the tiny front garden.

'That's yours?' he asked with a hint of awe.

'Yes. Is there somewhere I can put it?'

'In my garage next door. I'll show you the way.'

When the two men had vanished, Helen said, 'Well! So that's him! Noisy young fellow, isn't he?'

'He likes people to know he's there,' Sylvia said.

'Hmm! Not the retiring type, obviously.'

'Nobody could call Mark the retiring type,' Sylvia agreed, following her mother into the house.

In the better light Helen could see her daughter properly and was horrified.

'What are you wearing?' she demanded. 'What's that—thing in your hands?'

'I wear it on my head, and these are goggles to protect my eyes.'

'What do you want to go gadding around on that contraption, dressed like that for? To suit him?'

It was clear that Mark had got off on the wrong foot with Helen. With Joe, however, he had better luck. The motorbike had made an excellent impression and, as Dee watched them returning to the house, she could see that they were already in perfect accord.

'So now your dad's found someone to talk nuts and bolts with, he's happy,' Helen observed. 'I reckon that lad's got the job already.'

Then it happened. Mark threw back his head and roared with laughter, a rich, vibrant sound that streamed up to the heavens. It seemed to invade Dee through and through, filling her with helpless delight. All of life was in that sound; everything good and hopeful, all that was promising for the future. How could anything possibly go wrong with the world when a young man could laugh like that?

But then, mysteriously, she knew a flicker of alarm, as though a hidden danger was approaching her behind a smiling front. But it passed and she chided herself for being fanciful. Sylvia had found herself a pleasant young man. Surely all was well?

'Are you two coming in for your tea?' Helen called, and the two men obediently returned to the house.

Some instinct seemed to warn Mark that he was doing badly with Helen. He behaved charmingly, thanking her for allowing him to stay for Christmas.

'Any friend of Sylvia's is a friend of ours,' Helen said politely, and Dee might have imagined that she slightly emphasised 'friend'. 'Joe needs a good mechanic, so I hope things work out.'

'He *is* a good mechanic, Mum,' Sylvia said eagerly. 'The best.'

'Well, we'll see. It's almost teatime and I expect you're starving, Mr Sellon.'

'Please, call me Mark. And yes, I'm starving.'

'Come upstairs and unpack first,' Sylvia suggested. 'Where's he sleeping, Mum?'

'In Dee's room,' Helen said. 'She'll be in with you.'

'I thought Dee was going to sleep on the sofa down here,' Sylvia protested. 'That's what you said this morning.'

Helen dropped her voice to say, 'I've changed my mind. Now, get going and tea will be ready in a few minutes.'

At that moment Joe Parsons signalled for Mark to join

him in the sitting room. Sylvia went too and, when they were safely out of earshot, Helen said, 'If she thinks I'm letting her be alone in that room while he's here—well! That's all I can say.'

There was no need for her to say more. Her suspicions stood out brilliantly.

'You think he'd—you know—?'

'Not now, he won't,' Helen said with grim satisfaction.

'He's very good-looking, isn't he?' Dee ventured.

'Hmm. Handsome is as handsome does.'

'*Mum!* It's not his fault he's handsome.'

'Did I say it was? But they're the ones you have to watch, that's all. Now, go and lay the table.'

Over tea, Mark told them about himself. He was twenty-three and lived on the other side of London in a hostel for respectable young men. His father had died when he was six and he'd been reared by his mother alone.

'She had no family, and my father's family had disapproved of their marriage, so I don't think they helped her much. She died a couple of years ago.'

'So you've got nobody?' Helen asked with a touch of sympathy.

'Not really. I trained as a mechanic because my father was one. Luckily, I took to it and now I'm only happy with a spanner in my hand. I had a good job in a garage. At least I thought it was a good job, but the owner lost all his money, the garage was sold to someone who brought his own workforce in, and I was fired.'

'How did you get that motorbike?' Joe asked in a voice full of envy. 'Don't they cost a fortune?'

'Yes, they do,' Mark agreed, 'so I had to use rather un-usual methods. It belonged to the son of the man buying the garage. He wanted to sell it because he was getting a new one. I couldn't afford even the second-hand price, so I bet him he couldn't beat me at cards.' The gleam in his eyes had a touch of charming wickedness. 'And he couldn't.'

'No,' Joe breathed in awe. 'You're a bit of a devil, aren't you?'

'I hope so,' Mark said, sounding comically shocked. 'What's the point otherwise?'

'Hmm!' Helen said disapprovingly.

'I didn't cheat, Mrs Parsons,' Mark assured her. 'I just— tempted him a bit further than he'd meant to go.'

'That's what the devil does,' Dee said triumphantly, and was rewarded with his blazing grin that seemed to fill the room.

Helen frowned, disapproving. Sylvia looked as though she was struggling to keep up.

Afterwards, the men retired to the garage while the girls helped their mother in the kitchen.

'If you ask me, he's a bad lad,' Helen said.

'Why, Mum, whatever do you mean?' Sylvia asked.

'I mean he's the sort who goes around telling the world he's there all the time, like he did tonight. You watch out, my girl. Don't you go getting yourself into trouble.'

'Mum,' Dee protested, 'that's not fair. Sylvia's a good girl.'

Sylvia said nothing.

'Maybe she is, maybe she isn't,' Helen said. 'I'm taking no chances, not with him looking like he came off a cinema screen.'

'He is handsome, isn't he?' Sylvia said eagerly.

'Yes, he is—too handsome for his good or yours. That's why Dee's going to be with you in your room tonight. I don't want any of your nonsense.'

'Why, Mum, I don't know what you mean,' Sylvia said, earnestly enough to fool anyone who didn't know her.

'You know exactly what I mean, young lady. You behave yourself.'

Behind her mother's back, Sylvia made a face, but gave up arguing. Nobody won against Helen and they all knew it. When it was time to go to bed, she drew Mark aside in the hall, signalling for Deirdre to go on ahead.

Dee hesitated, mindful of her mother's orders to keep a strict eye on them. But Helen herself was only a few feet away in the kitchen and surely one little goodnight kiss couldn't do any harm?

'Go on,' Sylvia said urgently, jerking her head to the stairs and at last Dee obeyed, trying to sort out her thoughts.

There was another reason for her reluctance to leave them alone; one she couldn't admit to herself because she didn't fully understand it. It made no sense. After all, Mark was Sylvia's property.

Wasn't he?

Upstairs, she undressed slowly, trying not to let her mind dwell on the two lovers enjoying a tender embrace. In bed, she read for a little while, waiting for Sylvia to appear, but nothing happened.

When she could stand it no longer, she crept out into the hall and listened to the soft sounds coming from the bottom of the stairs, trying to picture what they would be doing.

Dee was a child of her time. At seventeen, she'd never known a passionate kiss, or even a non-passionate one. Nor had she seen one, unless you included Robert Taylor kissing Greta Garbo in the film of *Camille*. Apart from that, her knowledge of men and women was gleaned from her studies as a nurse, technical information that told her nothing of the passionate reality. About that she was as ignorant and innocent as any other respectable girl.

But tonight something had changed, making her aware of feelings and sensations that had existed beyond her consciousness. Mark had smiled at her, and he'd sat opposite her at the table, where she could see his face all the time. And nothing was the same. Now she was all avid curiosity to explore, but how could she? Mark was off-limits, and no other man existed.

From downstairs came a soft gasp followed by smothered laughter and a murmuring sound, telling of pleasure enjoyed to the full. Dee closed her eyes, her heart pounding, her breath coming in long gasps. She wanted—what? She couldn't tell. She only knew that she yearned for something above and beyond anything she'd known before.

From the kitchen came the sound of Helen banging pots and pans about, letting them know she was still there and they'd better stop what they were doing. Next moment Dee heard footsteps approaching and hurriedly retreated into the bedroom. By the time Sylvia came in, she was huddled down under the covers.

'Hello,' she murmured in a carefully sleepy voice. 'Have you said your goodnights?'

'Yes, thank you.' Sylvia sounded pleased with herself. 'What do you think of him?'

'He's all right. That motorbike is amazing, though.'

'Oh, the bike!' Sylvia said dismissively.

'I thought you liked it. It must be wonderful to ride with him.'

'Well, it isn't. I thought I was going to die. Of course I didn't tell him, he's so proud of it. You should hear him talk! He's just as bad about cars.'

'You don't sound as though you have much in common,' Dee observed casually.

'You wait until I get to work on him. He'll do anything for me. I'll have him just the way I want in no time.'

Dee didn't answer this, but something told her Sylvia was wrong. Beneath Mark's easy-going charm, she suspected a stubborn will to have his own way.

And yet, how could she tell? she wondered. What did she know of him, except that he was more good-looking than any man had the right to be, that he could make her laugh, and that his mind had a link with her own. At the table they had shared the 'devil' joke, which Sylvia hadn't understood, and that had been the sweetest moment.

More than sixty years later, it still lived in her mind.

I didn't know what had happened to me that night. I thought you were wonderful, but I had no idea of falling in love with you because I didn't know what love was. I only knew I was happy because you were going to stay with us for a few days. You dazzled me, and I didn't think there could be anything better in the world. That's how naive I was.

What is it, darling—are you restless? That's it, curl up against me and go back to sleep. That noise downstairs is them clearing up after the party. I suppose I ought to have offered to help, but I just wanted to be with you and think of all the things that have happened to us.

So many things—so many tears, so much laughter. So long ago, and yet not really a long time at all. I woke up next morning feeling so happy…

She had to be up very early to start work at the hospital and the day was still dark as she left the house, yet the world was mysteriously flooded with light.

At the bottom of the street was a bus stop, from which she could just see the front of the house, and the room that was normally hers. While waiting for the bus, she watched the window and saw it raised and Mark's head come out. He noticed her and waved. She waved back, feeling that the day had had a perfect start.

When she returned in the late afternoon, she saw Sylvia walking Billy in the street.

'I had to get out of the house,' she said crossly. 'Mark's spent the day in the garage with Dad and now neither of them can talk about anything but engines. Honestly! You'd think I didn't exist!'

'I suppose he has to think about engines some of the time,' Dee said mildly.

'Yes, but not when I'm there.'

'He's probably trying to impress Dad so that he can take this job and be near you.'

'Yes, that must be it,' Sylvia said, slightly mollified. 'But I'm going to find a way to get him out of the house tonight and have him all to myself.'

They had reached home by now. There was no sign of Mark, and Sylvia went looking for him. When she'd gone, he appeared so promptly that Dee was sure he'd been avoiding her.

'Is she still annoyed with me?' he whispered.

Mischievously, Dee nodded. 'You've been talking about engines all day, and that's a terrible crime.'

'Do all women find it boring?' he asked.

'Mostly, I suppose.'

'What about you? Doesn't a hospital need machines of some sort?'

'Yes, we do, and I'm learning how to work them, but I suppose it's more interesting if you're doing things yourself rather than just hearing about them.'

He pulled a face full of good-natured resignation, spreading his hands as if to say—what was he supposed to do?

'I keep getting it wrong,' he sighed. 'Sooner or later I always annoy women.'

She was about to tell him not to talk nonsense when she connected with the teasing look in his eye and in the same moment she was invaded by a sweet warmth that shook her to the soul.

'I can believe that,' she said in a voice that trembled slightly. 'In fact, I can't imagine how any woman puts up with you.'

'Neither can I,' he chuckled.

'Mark, are you there?'

Sylvia's voice brought them both back to reality. Dee

thought she spotted a brief look of exasperation on his face, but it vanished at the sight of her, smiling again and so lovely that Dee knew she herself was forgotten.

Supper was a cheerful meal. Joe was warm in his praise of Mark's abilities. The job offer was confirmed, and it was understood that he would stay with them until after Christmas, when he could start looking for a place of his own.

Afterwards, Sylvia announced that she and Mark were going to the cinema. 'There's that new film at the Odeon, *A Christmas Carol.* Mark's longing to see it.'

'Why, what a coincidence!' Helen exclaimed. 'Dee's been saying how much she wants to see it. You can all go together.'

'Mum, I can go another time,' Dee muttered, appalled by this blatant manipulation.

'Nonsense, you go now. You've been working hard. Clear off, the three of you. Have a good time.'

Sylvia seethed at having a chaperone forced on her. Dee was ready to sink into the ground at the suspicion of what Mark must be thinking. But when she dared to meet his eyes, she found them alive with fun.

Of course, she thought. He must have been in this situation a thousand times. The world was full of mothers trying to shield their daughters from his looks and charm.

She felt better. And the thought of an evening in his company was blissful. It was Sylvia who sulked.

CHAPTER THREE

IF MARK was annoyed at Dee playing gooseberry, he didn't show it. At the cinema he paid for her seat, placed her so that he was sitting between them and bought her an ice cream. When the lights went down, she sensed that he slipped his arm round the back of Sylvia's seat and turned his head in her direction.

After a while a woman in the row behind tapped him on the shoulder.

'Do you mind not leaning so close to your girlfriend?' she hissed indignantly. 'You're blocking my view.'

He apologised, and after that he behaved like a perfect gentleman.

When they left the cinema the lovers were in dreamily happy moods, but Dee was disgruntled.

'It was awful,' she complained. 'Not a bit like the book.'

'It's a film,' he objected mildly.

'But the book is by Charles Dickens,' she said, as though that settled the matter. 'And they changed things. The Ghost of Christmas Past was played by a girl, they cut out Scrooge's fiancée and—oh, lots of things.'

'Did they?' he asked blankly. 'I didn't notice. Does it matter?'

'Of course it matters,' she said urgently. 'Things should be done right.'

'Never mind her,' Sylvia said, peevish at having the romantic atmosphere dispelled. 'She's always finding fault.'

Mark grinned, his good temper unruffled. 'Hey, you're a real stickler, aren't you?' he challenged Dee.

'What's wrong with that?' she demanded.

'Nothing, nothing,' he said with comic haste. 'Just remind me not to get on your wrong side.'

Still clowning, he edged away from her, but added, 'I'm only joking.'

'Well, you shouldn't be,' Sylvia put in. 'People do get scared of Dee because she's always so grim and practical.'

'I'm not grim,' Dee said, trying to keep the hurt out of her voice, but failing.

Perhaps Mark heard it because he said quickly, 'Of course you're not. You just like to be precise and correct. Good for you. A nurse needs to be like that. Who'd want to be nursed by someone who was all waffly and emotional? I'll bet when you were at school, your best subjects were maths and science.'

'They were,' she said, warmed by his understanding.

'There you are, then. You've got what my father used to call a masculine mind.'

The warmth faded. He considered her precise, correct and unemotional, practically a man. And she was supposed to be flattered. But then, she thought sadly, he had no idea that his words hurt her. Nor did he care. He'd merely been spreading his charm around to avoid an argument. She pulled herself together and answered him lightly.

'You don't have to be a man to appreciate scientific advances. That film we saw tonight was in black and white, but one day they'll all be in colour.'

'Oh, come on!' Sylvia exclaimed cynically.

'No, she's right,' Mark said. 'They're making a film of *Gone with the Wind* right now, and I've heard that's in colour.'

'Yes, important films, with big stars,' Sylvia agreed. 'But

they'll never make ordinary films like that. It's too difficult and expensive. There are limits.'

'No, there aren't!' Dee said at once. 'There are no limits. Not just in films but in anything. In life. No limits.'

'You're just a little girl,' Sylvia said dismissively. 'You don't know what you're talking about.'

'Yes, she does,' Mark said. 'She's right about that. You can't live life to the full if you set limits on everything.'

From Sylvia's expression, it was clear that she didn't know what he was talking about and was simply exasperated with the pair of them. Mark slipped his arm comfortingly about her, but at the same time he gave Dee a wink that was…that was…she struggled for the right word.

Conspiratorial, that was it; a look that said they shared a secret knowledge that Sylvia couldn't understand.

Her heart soared again and she began to make plans for when they got home. She would lure him into a discussion about great matters—knowledge, life, no limits, and the mental bond they shared would grow firmer.

But, once inside, he yawned and said he was tired, which Dee didn't believe for a moment. There was no high-flown discussion, only a time of lying in the darkness knowing that Mark and Sylvia were downstairs, sharing a passionate good-night. Mental bonds were all very well, but they couldn't compete with Sylvia's curves or the come-hither look in her eye. It was a painful lesson in reality.

Christmas was getting closer. Mark started work in the garage, Sylvia was deluged with customers in the dress shop, but the one with the longest hours was Dee. Coming home late from the hospital one night, she fell asleep on the bus and woke to find Mark shaking her.

'When the bus came I could see you inside, fast asleep. You'd have been carried on, so we had to jump on and rouse you.'

'We?' she asked sleepily, looking around.

Then she realised that Billy was there, too.

'We went for a walk,' Mark explained. 'I saw the bus in the distance and I knew you were due home soon, so we waited at the stop.'

'What's that creature doing 'ere?' the conductor growled. 'He's dangerous.'

'He's not dangerous and we're just getting off,' Mark said, rising and pulling the cord.

'Not until you've paid your fare.'

Then things became comical because Mark had come out without money, and Dee had to pay for him. They descended onto the pavement, hysterical with mirth.

'I guess I'm not cut out to be a knight in shining armour, rescuing a damsel in distress,' he said. 'I'd leave the sword behind and have to borrow hers.'

'It's not your fault,' she protested. 'You didn't know you were going to need money when you came out. I expect even Sir Lancelot was short of four pence sometimes.'

'Which one was he?'

'The most famous one who sat at the Round Table. He flirted with King Arthur's wife Guinevere, and was banished in disgrace.'

'That sounds like me. Did he ever borrow money from Guinevere?'

'The legend doesn't say.'

'I expect he did. He probably took her to a café one evening and she had to pay for it.' He indicated a little café just up ahead. 'That would really annoy her, even if he promised to pay her back afterwards.'

'Very bad.' She nodded solemnly. 'She probably slammed his helmet down on his head. But she bought him a cup of tea afterwards.'

'But how could he drink it if his helmet was slammed down?' Mark wanted to know. 'She slipped up there.'

'I suppose he could raise it,' she mused. 'Unless, of course, it jammed.'

'Bound to, I should think.'

Exchanging ridiculous gobbledegook, they wandered on to the café. At the entrance he said, 'Maybe they won't let Billy in. I should have thought of that.'

'Don't worry. The owner is a friend of Dad's and he likes Billy.'

By lucky chance, Frank, the owner, was standing near the door. He ushered them in and fetched Billy a bowl of water before bringing them tea and buns.

'You won't tell anyone, will you?' Mark begged. 'My reputation would never recover.'

'What, that you drink something as unmanly as tea with two sugars? Of course not. Nothing less than a pint of beer for you.'

'That's not what I meant and you know it. If people found out that I had to let you pay for this, my reputation would never recover.'

'True,' she said in a considering voice. 'Perhaps I won't tell anyone just yet. I'll keep it in reserve to blackmail you with. I'll enjoy that.'

He grinned. 'That's all right, then.'

'Meaning that you think I wouldn't?'

'No, I'm sure you would. I've sized you up as a very tough character and I'm treading carefully. You scare me.'

'Oh, stop talking nonsense!' she chuckled, but in truth she didn't want him to stop. She wanted to sit here talking nonsense with him for ever.

'Yes, ma'am, no, ma'am, anything you say, ma'am. Shall I go down on one knee?'

'I'll chuck this tea over you in a minute.'

'That would be a waste after what you paid for it.'

That sent them both off in more gales of mirth, while Billy

glanced from one to the other with a look that said there was no understanding humans.

'Sylvia tells me you're on duty over Christmas,' he observed.

'Someone has to be. People still get sick.'

'But surely you're still a student?'

'Yes, but there are some things I can do. A dogsbody is always needed.'

He regarded her with admiration. 'Giving up Christmas to fetch and carry. Good for you. I couldn't do it. I like to enjoy myself, but I suppose you get your kicks out of doing good works.'

She made a face. 'Don't make me sound like some dreary embodiment of virtue. I don't want to work over Christmas either, but it's the job I've chosen. The dull bits are worth it for the wonderful bits. Good works, my foot!'

'I didn't mean to offend you.'

'Don't you put up with the dull bits of engines for the sake of the others?'

'There aren't any dull bits in my job. If there were, I wouldn't do it.'

'But life has dull bits. You can't opt out of them.'

'I can try. Live for the moment. Tomorrow may never come.'

'Do you know,' she said, suddenly struck, 'I hear a lot of people talking like that in the hospital. They're convinced there's going to be a war and they must make the most of what time they have now.'

'Very wise of them.'

'Does that mean you think there's going to be a war?' she asked seriously. 'People talk about it but—I just can't believe it.'

'Of course. Hasn't our Prime Minister assured us that Hitler is a man he can trust?'

He was referring to Neville Chamberlain who, following

Hitler's aggressive behaviour in Europe, had gone to meet him in September and returned, apparently reassured. Two weeks later he'd attended a conference with Hitler and signed an agreement accepting the annexation of the Sudetenland. On his return to England, he'd given a speech at the airport promising 'peace for our time'.

'It sounds all right,' Dee said, 'and yet—'

'And yet the government is already issuing gas masks and sending children away to the country for their own safety,' Mark continued. 'Does that look like peace in our time? Of course not. Winston Churchill was right.'

'Who's he?'

'An MP. He's always been a rebel voice and just now he's a bit of an outsider, but he talks a lot of sense. He said you can't make yourself safe by throwing a small country to the wolves. And he's right. We'll know in a few months.'

Until now, Dee had seen mainly Mark's flippant side. Hearing him talk in this serious way was almost like listening to a different man, but the very strangeness made her alert. She shivered. In a little while the skies might darken.

'Will you be drafted into the army?' she asked.

'I won't wait for that. I'll join the Air Force. I've always wanted to fly a plane and this could be my chance.' His eyes gleamed as though for a moment he'd forgotten everything but the hope of adventure.

'Yes, this could be your chance to get killed or horribly injured,' she said crossly.

He shrugged. 'That's the risk you take. The best fun always involves a risk.'

'Fun?' she said, aghast. 'The most terrible danger and you call it fun?'

'The more danger, the more fun,' he said irrepressibly.

'Surely there's more to life than fun?'

'Is there?' he asked innocently. 'What?'

She didn't try to answer. After all, he was right. There was no point in being gloomy. Enjoy the moment, especially if the moment could be spent like this, alone with him, enjoying all his attention, feeling their minds meet.

She guessed that he didn't share such understanding with Sylvia. Her attraction for him was something very different, nothing to do with minds or understanding. Tonight was special because it was hers, all hers.

'I don't suppose it will happen at all,' he said in a reassuring tone.

'That's not what you really think, is it?' she said. 'You're just trying to make the silly little girl stop worrying.'

'I don't think of you as a silly little girl,' he said seriously. 'How can you be? You're a nurse. People depend on you for their lives.'

'Then heaven help them!' she said wryly. 'Mr Royce says it'll be a long time before he'll put anyone's life in my hands because I'd only drop it.'

'Who's Mr Royce?'

'He's a surgeon at the hospital. He's given the students a couple of lectures. I asked him a question once. I thought it was quite clever, but as soon as the words were out I knew it was idiotic. He just looked at me wryly and shook his head. Afterwards, he told me to go and have a cup of tea. He said I looked as if I needed it. And I really did need it.'

'He didn't offer to buy it for you?'

'Goodness, no!' she said, shocked. 'He's the Great Man of the hospital. Students are beneath his notice, unless he's telling them how they did something wrong.'

'Does he tell you that often?'

'All the time. So does Matron, and the ward sisters. In fact, I'm just useless. I'll fail all my exams and probably have to go into the forces.' An imp of mischief made her add, 'Perhaps they'll let me join the Air Force. They say women will be allowed in very soon. I'll fly about the heavens and you can be my mechanic on the ground.' She giggled at the thought.

Mark listened with a sardonic expression. 'Be very careful what you say,' he warned. 'They may let women in the Air Force, but they will *not* let them fly, not if they have any sense. *You* will be *my* mechanic.'

'Aren't you afraid that I'll sabotage your engine?' she teased.

He assumed a lofty tone. 'On second thoughts, I think you should stay quietly in the kitchen, which is where a woman belongs. I don't know why we ever gave you the vote. All right, all right, don't eat me!'

He edged away, holding up his arms in a theatrical parody of self-defence.

'I've a good mind to set Billy on you,' she laughed.

'He wouldn't do it,' Mark observed. 'We're the best of friends.'

As if to confirm it, Billy put his nose on Mark's knee, gazing up at him worshipfully. Mark scratched his ears, returning a look that was almost as loving.

Dee was fascinated by this new side of him. His normal persona—cool, collected and humorous—had relaxed into the kind of daft adoration that dogs seemed able to inspire. She watched them for a while, smiling, until he looked up and coloured self-consciously.

'I always wanted a dog,' he said, 'but my mother wouldn't allow it. I tend to get rather stupid about other people's.'

'I don't think you're stupid because you like Billy,' she said. 'I'd think you were stupid if you didn't. When I set my heart on a dog my parents weren't keen either, but I pestered and pestered until they gave me Billy for my seventh birthday.'

'Pestering my mother would only have brought me a clip round the ear,' he said wryly. 'She didn't like what she called "insolence".'

'She sounds terrible.'

'No, she just had a very hard life. She was devastated after my father left.'

'I thought you said he died.'

'He did, eventually, but he deserted her first. Keep that to yourself, I don't tell everyone.'

She nodded, understanding the message that he hadn't told Sylvia.

'Unfortunately for us both,' he went on, 'I look very much like my father, and it didn't help.'

'She blamed you for that?' Dee demanded, aghast.

'It wasn't her fault,' Mark said quickly. 'She couldn't cope with her feelings, she didn't know what to do with me.'

'How old were you when your father left?'

'Six, and ten when he died.'

'No brothers or sisters?'

'No, I wish I had. It would have helped if there had been more of us. Or one of you,' he added, looking down at Billy. 'You'd have been a good friend.'

'She should have let you have a dog,' Dee said. 'You'd have been easier for her to cope with.'

'I got one once,' he said with a wry smile of recollection. 'It was a stray and quite small, so I took him home and hid him. I managed to keep him a secret for two days before my mother found out.'

'What did she do?' Dee asked, although she was afraid to hear.

'I came home from school one day and he'd vanished. I went through every room looking for him, but he wasn't there. She said he must have run away, but I found out afterwards that she'd thrown him out in the rain.'

'Did she give you a clip round the ear?'

'Mmm! But I was defiant. I went looking for him.'

'Did you ever find him?'

'Yes, I found his body in a pile of rubbish on the street. From the look of him, he'd starved to death.'

'Did you tell your mother?'

Mark shook his head.

She hesitated a moment before asking, 'Did she hit you often?'

'Now and then. When things got on top of her, she'd lash out. I learned to keep out of her way and stay quiet.'

Suddenly he raised his head. 'Hey, what is this? Why are we being so gloomy? It's way in the past, all over.'

She'd liked him before, but now she liked him even more for this brief glimpse into the unhappy childhood that must have made him as he was today. She guessed that it wasn't over, whatever he said.

'Nobody realised Billy was going to grow so enormous,' she said. 'He's really too big for that little house so I take him for walks whenever I can. Thank you for bringing him out.'

'He's marvellous company.' Frowning, he added, 'He must be about eleven, quite old.'

'Yes, I know I won't have him much longer so I make the most of every day. I can't bear to think of life without him.'

'I can imagine. He's exactly the dog I'd have liked.' Mark turned his attention back to Billy. 'D'you hear that? You've got a fan club right here.'

'I'm jealous,' Dee said, regarding Billy, who was receiving Mark's caresses with every sign of bliss. 'Normally he's only like that with me.'

'I guess he knows a willing slave when he sees one. Hey, the owner's trying to attract our attention. I think he wants to close.'

They took the journey home at a gentle stroll, enjoying the pleasant evening, which was mild for winter, with a bright sky. Once Mark stopped and gazed upwards, prompting her to say, 'Are you thinking of how soon you can be up there?'

'If there's a war. There might not be.'

'Then you'd have to forget planes and enjoy motorbikes. It must be thrilling to go at that speed.'

'I'll take you some time. Sylvia didn't like it, but I think you would.'

'Mmm, yes, *please!*'

He laughed and put a casual arm about her shoulders. 'You know, it's funny,' he mused. 'I've only known you a short time—but that's really all you need, isn't it?'

'Is it?' she asked breathlessly.

'Yes. I already feel that you're my best friend. I think I knew from the start, when we understood each other at once. Normally, a man wouldn't want a woman to understand him too well, but in you I like it. It's almost as though you're my sister. You don't mind my saying that, do you?'

'Not at all,' she said brightly. 'I've always wanted a brother.'

'Really? What a coincidence. I've often thought it would be nice to have a sister, preferably a younger one.'

'Yes, so that she could help you out of trouble without complaining, and let you get away with murder,' Dee said tartly.

He laughed. 'You see? You understand my requirements instinctively. What a fantastic sister to have!'

And she really *would* be his sister when he married Sylvia. With a sinking heart, she realised that he was preparing her for the announcement of the marriage.

Sylvia was waiting for them on the front step. 'Where have you been?' she demanded. 'You said you were taking Billy for a walk and you just vanished.'

He explained about rescuing Dee from the bus. 'So naturally I had to take her for a cup of tea.'

'That's right, I was dying for one,' Dee said. 'But Sir Lancelot rescued me.'

'Who?' Sylvia asked.

'Never mind,' Mark said, hastily drawing her aside.

Dee took Billy into the kitchen and released him from his lead while she explained to Helen.

'I hope that doesn't mean you don't want your tea,' her mother said practically. 'It'll be on the table in a minute.'

'I'm starving.'

On her way through the hall she was waylaid by Mark, hastily thrusting some money into her hand.

'That's too much,' she said, examining it.

'Give me the change later,' he muttered. 'Just don't tell—*Sylvia!*'

'What's going on?' Sylvia demanded, seeming to appear out of nowhere. 'Why are you giving Dee money?'

Quick as a flash, Dee replied, 'He's not giving it to me, he's lending it to me. I really try to manage on what I earn but I'm a bit short this week, so Mark's helping me out. Don't tell Mum, will you?'

'Of course not, but why didn't you ask me? I've helped you out before.'

'I know, and I didn't feel I could ask you again, and Mark's been *so* chivalrous.'

Somewhere in the atmosphere she was aware of Mark, torn in two directions; half of him grateful for her quick-witted rescue, the other half fighting to keep a straight face.

Sylvia remained oblivious to the undercurrents. 'You mustn't borrow money from Mark,' she said. 'It isn't proper. I'll lend you what you need. Now, give him that money back.'

'Yes, Sylvia,' she said meekly, handing the cash over but unable to meet Mark's eyes.

Nor could he meet hers. And somehow that made the secret all the sweeter.

It seems so trivial, looking back, but your masculine pride was involved, which made it important. I still laugh when I remember how horrified you were, and how we had to sneak a meeting later so that you could give me the money again. How grateful you were to me for putting Sylvia off the scent, and how happy I was!

Christmas was wonderful, just because you were there.

You gave us all presents, even Billy. He was overjoyed with that noisy toy you bought him and drove us all crazy with it, bless him! You gave Sylvia a pretty necklace, and me a purse saying it was 'to keep my money safe', putting your fingers over your lips. It meant the world to me that we shared a secret, even if you did spoil it a bit by saying, 'What a sister I have!'

That wasn't what I wanted to hear, but she could always take you away from me. She was the one you kissed under the mistletoe, while I looked away, then looked back. Seeing you like that hurt terribly, but I couldn't turn away again.

And then it was New Year's Eve, and that was when I discovered things I hadn't suspected before, things I didn't understand...

CHAPTER FOUR

As THE hands of the clock crept towards twelve on New Year's Eve, doors were flung open and the inhabitants of Crimea Street poured out into the open, carolling their pleasure up into the night sky.

'Goodbye, 'thirty-eight. Goodbye and good riddance!'

'Hello, 'thirty-nine. This is the year I'll get rich.'

'Listen to them,' Joe murmured. 'So sure it's all going to get better, when in fact—'

'Don't be so gloomy,' his wife advised him. 'There probably isn't going to be a war.'

'They said that just before the last one,' Joe said. 'Some of them were still saying it the day before I was drafted into the army.' He gazed sadly at the rapidly growing crowd, singing and dancing. 'They never think to wonder what the next New Year will be like,' he murmured.

'But we know what the next one will be like,' Dee said wryly. 'Mark and Sylvia will be married, and she'll probably be pregnant.'

'The way they're carrying on, it'll happen the other way round,' Helen observed grimly. 'Look at them. I didn't bring my girls up to act like that.'

Dee smothered a grin. Between her parents' wedding anniversary and Sylvia's birthday was a mere three months, but all the family pretended not to notice.

'*You* wouldn't do a thing like that, would you, Mum?' she asked demurely.

'That's enough from you, my girl. Any more of your cheek and I'll—'

'What, Mum?'

'And don't you think you can snigger and get away with it. Just you be careful.'

'Leave it,' Joe said easily. 'They're young, like we were once.'

He slipped his arm around his wife's shoulders. As she turned her head they exchanged smiles, and suddenly the staid middle-aged couple blurred and there was a faint echo of the young lovers whose passion had overcome them. Dee slipped quickly away.

She tried not to go in the direction of Mark and Sylvia, but she couldn't resist a quick look. As she'd feared, they were locked in each other's arms, oblivious to everyone around them, trusting the night and the excitement to conceal them.

How tightly he was holding her. How passionate his caresses, how tender his kiss. How Dee's heart yearned at the sight of her sister enjoying so much happiness in the arms of this wonderful young man.

She turned away, giving herself a firm lecture. She had no right to be jealous. He belonged to Sylvia. She would get over him and find someone who was right for herself.

But deep inside was the fear that this might never happen, that he was the one and only and she'd met him too late. He would be her brother-in-law, lost to her for ever, and she would become a mean, miserable old maid.

This prospect was so terrible that she forced a smile to her face and began to jump up and down, as if dancing.

'Come on, Dee,' yelled a voice in her ear. Arms went about her, sweeping her round and round.

It was Tom, who lived three doors down. He was gormless but well-meaning and she'd known him all her life, so she willingly danced with him and managed not to look at Mark and Sylvia for a while.

They danced and danced while someone played the accordion and fireworks flared. Then the cry went up, *'It's nearly midnight!'*

The cheers were deafening. *It's almost nineteen thirty-nine. Yippee!*

Laughing, Dee made the rounds of her friends and neighbours, hugging them, wishing them joy. Now she was looking out for Mark and Sylvia again, because surely she could sneak a New Year hug with him. Just sisterly, she promised herself.

In the distance she saw Sylvia and hurried towards her, but then she checked herself, unable to believe what she'd seen.

Her sister was in a man's arms, but the man wasn't Mark.

Nonsense, it *must* be Mark! Who else could it be?

But it wasn't Mark. It was the new milkman.

Never mind, she tried to reassure herself. Just a neighbourly embrace; nothing more.

But it was far more. Sylvia's mouth was locked on the young man's as firmly as it had been locked on Mark's just a few minutes ago.

Firecrackers exploded all around her. The sky was brilliant, but inside her there was darkness. Sylvia had betrayed Mark, had turned from his arms to another man. *How could she?*

Turning, she could see Mark, looking around him as though trying to find Sylvia. She hastened over to him, calling his name and forcing him to turn so that he couldn't see into the shadows, and the heartbreak that awaited him there.

'Dee!' he called cheerfully. 'Come here!'

Before she knew it, he seized her by the waist, raised her high above his head, holding her as easily as if she weighed nothing, then lowered her to deliver a smacking kiss. It was the act of a friend, not a lover. Yet her heart leapt at the feel of his mouth against hers. If only it would last! If only it could be for real!

But it was over. She knew a sad feeling of irony as her feet touched the ground. This was where she belonged. Not up in the air.

'Have you seen Sylvia?' he asked.

'I…no, I…thought she'd be with you.'

'She was, but someone grabbed her and danced her away.'

'And you're not jealous?'

'Because she dances with another fellow? I'm not that pathetic.'

His grin was full of cheeky self-confidence, saying that he had nothing to fear. It plainly never occurred to him that Sylvia might have crossed the line.

Only later did Dee realise that she could have seized the chance to reveal Sylvia's treachery to Mark and break them up, perhaps claim him for herself. At the time, all she could think was that he must be protected from hurt.

'Come on, let's dance,' he said, opening his arms.

It was bliss to dance with him, feeling his arms about her, knowing that the other girls envied her. News of his attractions had gone around the neighbourhood like lightning and everyone wanted to see him. Having seen him, they wanted to stay and see some more, and then to dance with him.

One or two of them tried to break in, claiming to believe that this was an 'excuse me' dance. Dee suppressed the inclination to do murder, swung away to another partner, but then reclaimed Mark as soon as possible.

'You're putting me in danger,' he joked breathlessly as they bounded around together. 'There are at least three men who thought you should turn to them, but you came to me. I'm flattered.'

'Don't be. I'm just keeping Sylvia's property safe for her. I'm a very good sister.'

'Her sister or mine?'

A mysterious instinct to confront the thing she dreaded made her say, 'It's going to be the same thing soon, isn't it?'

His face darkened. 'Who can tell? Where is she?'

'Why don't you go and find her?'

His lips twisted wryly, and she understood the message. Mark Sellon did not search yearningly for a woman, or beg for her attention. He let them beg him.

'You're the only one she cares about,' Dee urged. 'She's probably just trying to make you jealous.'

'Then she's failing,' he said lightly. 'Let's go.'

He swung her higher in the air but, before he could do more, they both saw Sylvia on the edge of the crowd. She was with a different young man, struggling with him, although not seriously, and laughing all the while. She laughed even louder when he managed to plant a kiss on her mouth.

Suddenly Dee found herself alone. There was a yell from the young man as he was hauled away and dumped on the pavement, and a shriek of excitement from Sylvia as Mark hurried her unceremoniously down a side street and into the darkness. The fascinated onlookers could just make out raised voices, which stopped very suddenly.

'No prizes for guessing what's happening now,' someone said to a general laugh.

But then they all fell silent as the church clock began to strike midnight, looking up into the sky as though they could read there the tale of the coming year.

He'll marry her, Dee thought forlornly, *and I'll have to move away so that I don't see him so much. Perhaps I could move into the Nurses' Home.*

'Hey, Dee!' Helen and Joe were waving, beckoning for her to join them as the clock neared twelve.

'Where's Sylvia?' Helen demanded. 'Ah, yes, I can see her.'

There she was, drifting slowly back along the street, arms

around Mark, her head resting on his shoulder, gazing up at him with a look of adoration; a look he returned in full. As the clock reached the final 'bong' he pulled her into a tight embrace, crushing her mouth with his own as the crowd erupted around them.

'*It's nineteen thirty-nine!*'

'*Happy New Year!*'

'*Happy New Year, everybody! Happy—happy—happy—*'

Mark and Sylvia heard none of it. At one with each other, they had banished the world. Nothing and nobody else existed.

'Including me,' Dee whispered softly. 'Happy New Year.'

Two days later, Mark moved out to a local bed and breakfast, and after that Dee saw less of him. They would sometimes pass as she was leaving for work and he was just arriving at the garage, but she was usually home too late to catch him. Once a week Sylvia would bring him to supper. Other nights she would go out and return late. Watching jealously, Dee saw that sometimes she came home smiling, and sometimes she seemed grumpy, but she always denied that there had been any quarrel.

Dee constantly braced herself for news of the engagement, but it never came. As the weeks passed, her nerves became more strained until it would almost have been a relief to know that he'd finally proposed to Sylvia, even set the date. If only it would happen soon, before she fell totally in love with him and it was too late.

And all the time she knew she was fooling herself. The spark of love had ignited in her the night they'd met, but she'd been too inexperienced to know it. Over the next few days it had flared and grown stronger. Now it was already too late. It had always been too late. It had been too late from the first moment.

Day after day, she waited for the axe to fall but, mysteriously, it never did.

There wasn't always time to worry about her own life. As the early months of 1939 passed, the news from Europe grew more ominous and war more likely. Hitler continued to invade weaker countries, annexing them in defiance of the Munich Agreement that he'd signed with Neville Chamberlain the previous September, until even Chamberlain announced that negotiations with him were impossible.

'Mark can't talk about anything else,' Sylvia said sulkily. 'He's set his heart on the Air Force, and he just takes it for granted that I'll stick around.'

'But of course,' Dee said, shocked. 'You couldn't leave him when he was doing his duty to his country.'

'To him it's fun, not duty. I can't even get his attention long enough to make him jealous.'

'Is that what you've been trying to do?' Dee asked curiously.

'Just a little. It worked at New Year but—oh, I don't know. I have to make him realise that I'm here and he's got to notice me.'

'Don't do anything stupid,' Dee warned.

Sylvia's response was a wry look that she didn't understand until later.

Tom, the young man from three doors down who'd danced with Dee on New Year's Eve, began to invite her out. Without encouraging him too much, she agreed to the odd trip to the cinema because she was blowed if she was going to spend her time pining for Mark Sellon, thank you very much!

Tom wasn't brainy, but he had a cheeky humour that appealed to her. Laughing with him wasn't the same as laughing with Mark. There was none of the edgy excitement that made it so much more than humour. But Tom could tell a joke well, and they were chuckling together the night they arrived at her home to find Mark there, looking troubled.

'Is something the matter?' Dee asked quickly.

'No, I'm just waiting for Sylvia. She's a bit late tonight.'

'I thought she was meeting you in town,' Dee said, frowning.

'Did she say that?' Mark said easily. 'I must have got it wrong. Sorry to trouble you.' He was out of the door before they could reply.

'Your sister's got them all running around after her,' Tom said admiringly.

'Funny,' Dee mused. 'I'm sure she said she wasn't coming home early. Oh, well.'

Looking back, it was easy to see this as the first ominous sign. The second came later that night when Sylvia returned, beaming and cheerful, and seemed delighted to know Mark had been looking for her.

'Was he very upset?'

'He certainly wasn't happy. Do you *want* him to be upset?'

Sylvia shrugged. 'It won't do him any harm to worry about me for a change. He winks at every girl who passes.'

'But that's just his way.'

There was a brief pause before Sylvia said, 'That's what I used to believe, but now I think it's more than just a bit of harmless fun. There's something in him—something I can't reach because he won't let me. He seems so outgoing and friendly but it's an illusion. He keeps the important part of himself hidden. He'll flirt and play the passionate lover, but that's not love. Not really. He doesn't like getting close in other ways.'

'Perhaps he doesn't trust the idea of love,' Dee said thoughtfully.

'Why should you say that?'

'I mean after what happened in his childhood—his father leaving and his mother being so withdrawn, you know.'

'No, I don't know. What are you talking about?'

So Mark hadn't told Sylvia what he'd told her, Dee realised. He'd hinted as much but she'd thought that resolution would change as he grew closer to her sister. But it seemed they hadn't grown closer at all.

'Maybe I'd better ask Mark,' Sylvia said shrewdly.

'No,' Dee said quickly. 'I wasn't supposed to repeat it. I forgot. It's just that—'

Briefly, she outlined what he'd told her about his lonely childhood, and the dog his selfish mother had got rid of without even telling him.

'That woman sounds hateful,' she finished. 'However unhappy she was, she had no right to take it out on a child. No wonder he grew up cautious about getting close to people.'

'So that's why he doesn't open up to anyone,' Sylvia mused. 'Including me. But it seems he talks to you.'

'Because he sees me as a sister. A sister can't hurt him like you can, so he feels safe talking to me. But don't tell him I told you.'

'All right, I promise. I'll keep hoping that he'll tell me himself, but he won't, I know that in my heart. You see, I don't matter to him, or not very much. The other night we were going to meet for a date, and he was nearly an hour late. He made some excuse but I think he was with another girl. I'm sure I could smell her perfume.'

'You're imagining things,' Dee said, unwilling to believe the worst of Mark.

'Am I? Maybe. But I resent the time I spend worrying about him. I once thought that he and I would walk off into the sunset and live happily ever after. But now—' She gave an awkward laugh. 'If I don't matter to him, there are plenty of other men who think I matter. I'm going to bed. Goodnight.'

When Dee finally went to her own room she was puzzled. Whatever Sylvia said, Mark was surely under her spell, even if it was only her physical beauty that had drawn him there. She recalled her mother's teaching on the subject.

'They all start off wanting just one thing,' Helen had said. 'A clever woman uses that to get a ring on her finger.'

It was the wisdom of the time. Any woman of Helen's generation, or even Dee's generation, would have said the same. The idea of risking the wedding ring by playing fast and loose with his affections was sheer madness. Dee knew that she could never have done so if she'd been lucky enough to entrance Mark.

'But that's not going to happen,' she told her reflection. 'He's never going to gaze at you as if the sun rose and set on you, so shut up, go to bed, forget him and get on with your life.'

Sometimes lecturing herself helped. Mostly, it didn't.

What did help was walking in the evening with Billy, now their mutual friend. 'You're crazy about him too, aren't you?' she asked the dog as they strolled along.

Billy gave a soft grunt of agreement. The next moment it had turned into a yelp of delight as a motorbike turned the corner of the road. Even in goggles, it was clearly Mark, and Billy shot ahead so fast that the lead slipped out of Dee's hand.

'Billy, no!' she shrieked as the dog went bounding into the road, straight into the path of the speeding motorbike, and to inevitable disaster.

It was all over in a flash. One moment the bike was bearing down on the dog; the next moment there was a crash and a yell as the vehicle swerved violently and smashed into a fence. Mark was flung to the ground and lay still.

'Oh, no!' Dee whispered, running towards him and dropping to her knees beside his frighteningly still form. 'Mark! *Mark!*'

'I'm all right,' he murmured. 'Go and catch that daft animal before he gets killed.'

Catching Billy was easy as he'd come to a halt, staring at

the mayhem he'd caused and whining. As she secured his lead,
Mark was already rising painfully from the ground.

'Are you hurt?' Dee begged.

'No, just a few bruises,' he gasped, rubbing himself.

Doors opened. People came running out. Sylvia had seen
everything through a window and was weeping as she threw
her arms around him.

'I'm all right,' he said, staggering slightly.

Sylvia turned on Dee in fury. 'Why don't you keep that
animal under control? Mark could have been killed.'

'But I wasn't,' he said. 'It's not Billy's fault.'

'No, it was mine,' Dee said quickly. 'I'm sorry. Don't stay
out here. Let's get inside quickly.'

Leaning on Sylvia, he walked slowly into the house and
sat thankfully on the sofa, throwing his head right back, eyes
closed.

'Let me have a look at you,' Dee said.

'I've told you, I'm fine.'

For once she lost her temper. '*I'm* the nurse,' she snapped.
'*I'll* say if you're fine.'

That made him open his eyes. 'All right, nurse. All right,
all right. Whatever you say.'

She gave him a sulphurous look and started undoing the
contraption he wore on his head. It was made of some light
metal, barely covering his hair, and if he'd landed on his head
it wouldn't have protected him, but luckily he hadn't. His
shoulder had taken the full impact.

'Fine, let me see your shoulder,' she said, becoming busi-
nesslike.

Between them, she and Sylvia eased off his jacket, then
his shirt, revealing bruises that were already turning a nasty
colour.

'Now your vest,' she said. 'I want to see your ribs. That's
it, now lean forward so that I can see the back.'

There were more bruises, but nothing was broken.

'You don't know how lucky you are,' Dee said. 'But I'd like you to come into Accident and Emergency at the hospital tomorrow and they'll take some X-rays.'

'What for?' he demanded with cheerful belligerence. 'I've had the best nurse in the business. If you say I'm all right, then I am.'

'Yes, but—'

'Stop making a fuss, Nurse.'

'Put your clothes on,' Sylvia said.

Something in her voice, perhaps a tense note, made Dee suddenly realise that Sylvia was jealous. She didn't like anyone else to see Mark's bare chest. Nor did she like Dee being free to touch it.

The knowledge was like a light coming on, revealing what she hadn't seen before, that Mark's lean muscularity was as eye-catching as the rest of him. Functioning solely as a nurse, she'd run her hands professionally over that smooth torso, sensing only its medical condition. Now she wondered how she could have failed to notice the rich sheen of his skin, the faint swell of muscles that were strong but not over-developed.

But that was forbidden thinking, so she turned away, saying gruffly, 'Sylvia will help you get dressed.'

Joe came in from the garage where he'd been examining the bike.

'How is it?' Mark asked quickly.

Joe sighed and shook his head. 'Not good. The wheel's bent and there's plenty of other damage.'

Mark groaned.

'It's my fault,' Dee said. 'If I'd kept better hold of Billy's lead, it wouldn't have happened. I'll pay for any repairs.'

'I don't think it can be put right,' Joe told her.

'Then I'll replace it,' she said stubbornly.

'Dee,' Mark said, 'sweet, innocent Dee, it would take you a year's salary to buy another. Forget it.'

'But that bike was your pride and joy and I've ruined it,' she protested.

'So, it's ruined. That's life. Easy come, easy go. I only acquired it in the first place through being thoroughly devious. Something else will come along and I'll be devious again. Don't worry. It comes naturally to me.'

There was a growl of rage and a middle-aged man thrust his way into the room. With a groan Dee recognised Jack Hammond, the neighbour whose fence Mark had smashed, and who was bad-tempered even at the best of times.

'Do you know what you've done to my fence?' he shouted.

'Sorry about that,' Mark said. 'I'll mend it.'

'I should think you will. Why the devil did you have to swerve?'

Mark sighed. 'Because otherwise I'd have killed the dog,' he said, like a man explaining to an idiot.

'So what? It would have been his own fault.'

'Sure. I wonder why I didn't think of that,' Mark said ironically. 'It would have made everything all right, wouldn't it? I've told you I'll mend the fence.'

'You'd better.'

From the corner came a whimper. Billy was sitting there, looking apprehensive, as though he understood.

'You should put that creature down,' Hammond snapped. 'I've a good mind to—'

He didn't finish the sentence. Mark had struggled to his feet, wincing but determined, and confronted Hammond fiercely.

'Leave Billy alone,' he grated. 'I don't even want to see you looking at him. Now get out of here before I make you sorry.'

'Oh, so now you're—'

'Get out!'

Hammond didn't argue further. He knew murder in a man's eyes when he saw it. He fled.

Mark collapsed back onto the sofa and held out his hand to Billy. 'Come here.'

Apprehensively, the dog came to him. Dee held her breath.

'You daft mutt,' Mark said in a mixture of exasperation and affection. 'You crazy, stupid animal; have you got a death wish? You could have been killed back there, do you realise that? Of all the—' Words seemed to fail him. 'Will you be sensible next time? Do you know how?'

Billy whined softly.

'No, you don't,' Mark said. 'Nor do I, according to some people.' He put an arm around the dog. 'Don't worry; it's all over now. But don't take any more silly risks because *she*—' indicating Dee '—can't do without you.'

'Considering he nearly killed *you*—' Helen said, amazed.

'That's all right. I can take care of myself. He can't. He's an idiot.' But, as he said it, he enveloped Billy in a bear hug. Dee barely saw it through her tears.

It was settled that he would stay the night. Dee's room was cleared for him and she moved in with Sylvia, as she'd done last time. She produced some liniment to rub into the bruises, but Sylvia snatched it out of her hand and insisted on doing it herself.

She spent some time comforting Billy, reflecting on Mark's comment that she couldn't do without him. He was right, of course. She wondered how many men would have swerved and accepted injury to themselves rather than hurt an elderly mongrel. He might play the giddy charmer, but this was the real man, she was sure of it.

In her mind she saw him again, bare-chested, lean, strong, powerful. Her hands seemed to tingle with the memory of touching him and an equation began to hammer on her brain, demanding entrance.

Medical condition: satisfactory.

Personal condition: a million times more than satisfactory.

Go to bed, she told herself crossly. And pull yourself together. Remember you're a nurse.

She slept for a few hours and awoke to hear Sylvia getting out of bed and creeping out of the room. She slipped out after her and reached the corridor in time to see her sister go into Mark's room. The whispers just reached her.

'I came to see if the patient's all right.'

'All the better for seeing you,' he said.

'Let's see if I can make you feel better.'

Standing in the bleak corridor, Dee heard muffled laughter ending in his exclamation of, 'Ow! Be careful. I'm delicate.' More laughter.

She crept back to her room and closed the door.

Next morning, she rose early. Even so, he was down before her, in the garden with Billy. She found them sitting quietly together, his hand on the dog's head.

'Have you managed to reassure him yet?' she asked.

'Just about.'

'Mark, I don't know how to thank you for being so nice about this, not just about the bike, but about Billy.'

'Let it go. It wasn't his fault. But listen, keep him indoors for a while. In fact, I'll take him into the garage with me.'

'You think Hammond—?'

'I don't know, but I didn't like the look on his face last night.'

'I do wish you'd come to the hospital—'

But his serious mood had passed and he waved her to silence. 'Who needs a hospital when they've had you looking after them? I didn't hit my head. Look—' he leaned forward for her inspection '—nothing there.'

'That's certainly true,' she said wryly. 'Nothing there at all. Outside or in.'

He grinned. 'I see you understand me. Are you cross with me?'

'How can I be when you were so generous about it? Especially to Billy. But I will help out with the money and—'

'No need. I'll probably get something from the insurance.'

'But if it's not enough, I'll—'

'That's it. This conversation is over. Isn't it time for breakfast? Come along, Billy.'

Man and dog strode into the house, leaving her gazing after them, exasperated and happy.

You barely got anything from the insurance company, did you? Not enough to buy another motorbike, but you didn't tell me. You simply said you'd changed your mind about having one. I might have believed you, but Dad was there when the inspector came and he told me afterwards. I tried to speak of it but you got really cross. It's funny how there were some things you just couldn't cope with. Sometimes you seemed happier with Billy than anyone else. You didn't have to put on a performance with him.

Or with me. That was the nicest thing.

CHAPTER FIVE

Dee's eighteenth birthday was approaching. There would be a party with all the neighbours and for a few hours everyone would forget the approaching war.

On the night, Mark came to meet her at the bus stop.

'I'm the delegation sent to escort you home,' he said cheerfully. 'Your dad let me leave work a little early so that I could shift the furniture for your mum and help her put up the decorations. She's baking a cake for you—the best cake ever, with eighteen candles.'

'Mum always does the best cake ever,' Dee chuckled. 'For Sylvia's twentieth she produced a real masterpiece. Is Sylvia home yet, by the way?'

'Not yet. She'll be along soon.'

As they neared the front door they could see the first guests arriving, everyone waving as they saw each other. Laughing, they all hurried in. After that, the bell rang every few minutes and soon the place was full. Except for Sylvia.

'We're not waiting for anyone,' Helen declared. 'This is your evening. Let's get on with it.'

There were cards and presents to be opened, laughter to be shared. Afterwards, Dee vaguely recalled these things, but the details blurred in the shock of what came afterwards. Neither she, her parents, nor Mark, would ever quite recover from that shock.

She had slipped into the hall, meaning to fetch something

from upstairs, when she noticed an envelope lying on the mat. With a sense of foreboding, she saw that the handwriting was Sylvia's.

She tore it open, telling herself that her worst fears were realised, but even her worst fears hadn't prepared her for what she found.

I'm sorry to do this now, but I shan't be there this evening. I've gone away for a long time, maybe for good. I'm in love and I have to be with Phil, no matter what else it means.

A friend has delivered this, so don't look for me outside the door. I'm already far away.

Say sorry to Mark for me. I didn't mean to do it this way. Try to make him understand and forgive me. He doesn't love me really, and he'll get over it.
Love, Sylvia

She read it again and again, trying to understand that it was real and not some wicked joke. Then life returned to her limbs and she tore open the front door, running out in a frantic search for whoever might have thrust this through the letterbox. But the street was empty in both directions.

Her head spinning, she stumbled back to the house and leaned against the wall, shaking. Mark came out and found her like that.

'You're being a long time. Everyone's asking what—Dee, what is it?'

'Sylvia,' she said hoarsely.

He took the note from her hand and read it.

'Well,' he said heartily, 'so that's that.'

But she wasn't fooled. She'd glanced up just in time to see his expression in the split second before the mask came down, and she'd never seen such devastation in any man's face. He actually seemed to wither, mouth growing pinched, eyes closing as if to shut out intolerable pain. The next moment he opened them again and smiled. But the smile only touched his mouth. His eyes were blank.

'She just vanished without a goodbye,' he whispered.

'Mark, I'm so sorry,' she whispered.

He raised his head. His face was set. 'Sorry? What for? Sylvia has the right to do as she pleases. We weren't engaged or anything like that.'

'But to do it like this—'

'Not very polite, but if she wants to be with him—' His voice shook and for a moment he shuddered uncontrollably.

'Dee, are you coming back in?' It was her mother's voice, approaching.

Swiftly, Mark put the letter into his pocket.

'Say nothing until the party's over,' he said.

He was right. She wilted at the thought of telling her parents about this. Their eyes met and they each took a deep breath before heading back into the house.

Someone had brought a gramophone and a collection of dance records, which mercifully made talk impossible for some time. But there was no hiding the way people looked at Mark, or the almost tangible curiosity about Sylvia's absence.

And how they would laugh, she thought angrily. Mark's popularity had always contained a touch of jealousy, even spite. Every girl who'd yearned for him, every young man who'd envied him, would relish seeing him undermined now.

A fierce desire to protect him made her grasp his hand, saying, 'Dance with me, Mark. It's my birthday, and I get to choose.'

He seized her with what might have been eagerness, but she sensed mainly relief that with her he could briefly drop the bright mask.

I wonder where Sylvia's got to. Do you think Mark knows?

The words floated indistinctly through the crowd. Impossible to say who'd uttered them, and nor did it matter.

'Ignore that,' she told him. 'The fact is, you knew Sylvia wasn't going to be here, and you're completely relaxed about it.'

'Am I?'

'All you can think about now is enjoying yourself with me,' she persisted, meeting his eyes urgently and trying to convey her message. 'Hold me close and look deep into my eyes, as though I was all you cared about in the world.'

If only...

He nodded, understanding and following her lead with a good deal of skill. The house was tiny and 'dancing' consisted mainly of taking small steps from side to side, but that, too, was useful, because their 'audience' had a close-up view of the performance.

'Smile,' she whispered, favouring him with a dazzling smile of her own. 'Pretend I'm Sylvia.'

He managed to stretch his lips, although his eyes were still blank. Dee raised her head so that her mouth was closer to his, not kissing, but conveying the impression that she would kiss him if they were alone.

Suddenly she clutched her head and said, 'Oh, I've got such a headache.'

'It's getting late,' Helen said. 'It's been a nice evening, but—'

Obediently, everyone began to drift off. It wasn't really late at all, but everyone knew 'something was up'.

'Shame Sylvia couldn't make it,' someone murmured. 'I wonder what kept her.'

There were several curious looks at Mark, then everyone was gone.

'Right, what is it?' Helen demanded, looking from one to the other. 'What are you two keeping a secret?'

'Sylvia's gone away, Mum,' Dee said. 'She left a letter.'

Mark handed it over and Helen read it, her face becoming like stone.

'She's with a man,' she said harshly. 'My daughter's a bad girl?' She glared at Mark. 'What do you know about this? Why didn't you stop her?'

'Because I didn't know.'

'You're supposed to have been courting her all this time. Why didn't you protect her?'

Dee forced herself to be silent. She longed to cry out that someone should have protected Mark from Sylvia's treachery, but he would have hated that. She contented herself with saying, 'Why don't you save your anger for Phil?'

'Just who is he?' Helen demanded.

'I think I saw him once, when I went to collect her from the shop,' Mark said. 'They were giggling together. We had a row about it.'

Suddenly Helen burst into sobs. Dee moved towards her, but her father appeared from the doorway where he'd been hovering and signalled for them to go. She left them in each other's arms, while she and Mark went out into the garden.

Once outside, Mark leaned against the wall, dazed like a man in a nightmare.

'We can't just leave it there,' he said. 'I have to find her, but I don't know how.'

'She said she was already far away,' Dee recalled. 'They'll probably know more at the shop. It's my half-day tomorrow. I'll go over and see what I can find out.'

'Shall I come with you?' he asked quietly.

She knew what it cost him to make the suggestion, for she felt everything with him: the pain of revealing himself as the rejected one, the shame of admitting how he'd been deceived, the awareness of smothered grins. Her heart ached for him.

'It's best if I go alone,' she assured him. 'They'll talk more freely to me.'

'Thank you.' That was all he said, but she knew he'd divined her understanding and was grateful.

She went to the shop the next day and returned home that evening with a heavy heart.

'They all know Phil,' she said. 'He's the rep for a clothing firm so he was in and out quite a lot, and they got to know each other.'

'But why did they run away?' Helen asked wretchedly. 'Why not just get married?'

'They can't,' Dee said reluctantly. 'It seems that Phil is already married.'

Helen gave a little scream and covered her face. Joe grew pale and said, 'I don't believe it. A married man, and she's living with him. She wouldn't do anything so wicked.'

'I'm afraid it's true,' Dee said. 'His wife was in the shop when I arrived. She'd come looking for him. They have two children and he seems to have just left them all.'

She was giving them only half the story, but there was no way she could tell them about the other things she'd learned—about Sylvia's reputation as a minx who routinely flirted with any man, and perhaps more. His abandoned wife had gone further, calling Sylvia a prostitute, but this, too, she would always keep to herself.

At last Helen dropped her hands and lifted her head. Her face was hard. 'She's no daughter of mine,' she said. 'As far as I'm concerned, she's dead.'

'Mum!' Dee protested.

'She never sets foot in this house again. She's not my daughter.'

Dee turned to her father.

'I don't know,' he said helplessly. 'Perhaps your mother knows best. Sylvia has put us out of her life.'

'But maybe she'll need our help.'

'She's dead to me,' Helen said stonily. She rose and kissed

Dee's cheek. 'You are my only daughter now. Remember that.'

She stalked out of the room, followed by Joe.

'I'm going out,' Mark said. 'I need to get drunk.'

'Let me come with you. We'll get drunk together.'

She had no intention of drinking, but she wasn't going to turn him loose upon the world in his present state. Taking him firmly by the hand, she led him out of the house. She, too, was in shock, but she'd had time to think about things on the way home. Mark was still stunned. When he spoke, it was in short, jerky sentences.

'How long has it been going on?' he asked.

'I…can't say,' she said, not entirely truthfully.

'Tell me,' he said violently. 'Don't spare my feelings. I want to know the truth, however bad.'

The truth was that Sylvia had been playing them off against each other for at least two months, perhaps longer. Dee had encountered Philip Mason once, a burly man in his thirties, pleasant enough but uninspiring. How Sylvia could have preferred him to the dashing Mark baffled her.

'It was a few weeks,' she said vaguely.

'And I thought she loved me. I respected her, do you know that? I thought she was a decent girl and I didn't…well, anyway, I respected her. And all the time she was…well…'

They walked on in silence for a while. Dee had tucked her hand into the crook of his arm and kept it there determinedly, lest he escape and do something that might harm him.

'Don't brood about it,' she begged. 'It can't do any good now.'

'It might teach me to be more wary of girls another time. How everyone will laugh at me.'

To comfort him, she denied it, but her words were hollow. Their performance at the party would help only for a short time. The truth would soon seep out.

'They don't matter,' she said urgently. 'You must thumb

your nose at them. All they need to know is that you and Sylvia have split up—'

'Because she preferred someone else.'

'No, she pretended to prefer someone else because she knew you'd lost interest.'

'Who'll believe that?'

This was what Dee had been preparing for, when she must risk everything on one throw of the dice. To the last moment she wasn't sure if she had the nerve, but then she took a deep breath and threw her fate to the winds.

'Everyone will believe it,' she said, 'if you're seen with another girl.'

'But how can I do that to any girl—deceive her into thinking I'm interested when I'm just playing a part?'

'But if she already knew the truth, you wouldn't have to deceive her,' Dee pointed out.

'But who would—?' He stopped as her meaning started to get through to him. 'Are you saying that you'd be willing to—?'

'It can't be anyone but me,' she said. 'You said once I was your best friend. Well, friends help each other out. One day I'll ask you to do something for me.'

'Is that a promise?' he demanded harshly. 'Because I must give you something back.'

'It's a promise.'

'I still don't understand. How do we go about this?'

'Look down that road,' she said, pointing. 'Those three people coming this way were at the party. Now they're turning into The Dancing Duck, so we'll go there, too.'

'They'll be our first audience,' he said, catching her mood.

'That's right. They're looking at us. Put your arm around my shoulders—that's it! Are you ready?'

'Quite ready. Sound the bugles! Forward march!'

Defiantly, they raised their heads and walked on into battle.

Eyes turned towards them as they went into the public house. Apparently unaware, they found a corner table and sat talking quietly while he sipped a beer and she an orange juice.

She knew, because Sylvia had told her, that they had often come here together, sometimes alone, sometimes in a group of their friends, the very ones who were glancing at them now, while trying to seem as if they weren't.

'Come to think of it, there was always something slightly wrong between us,' Mark brooded. 'She was so beautiful and I wanted her like mad, but we never seemed to talk about much. Not that we needed much talking, but when we did—I don't know—there was nothing there. I kept meaning to back away, but then she'd give me that look and I'd melt.'

'I know,' she said softly.

'You do?'

'I saw you melt.'

'Yes, you don't say much, but you see a lot more than most people, don't you? You saw what a fool I was.'

'You weren't a fool,' she insisted. 'Everyone gets carried away by their feelings sometimes.'

'Not you, I'll bet,' he said with a faint friendly grin.

'I'm just eighteen; there hasn't been time,' she said with an air of primness.

'That's not the reason. You've got your feet on the ground, not like the rest of us.'

My feet aren't on the ground, she thought. *I'm floating on air because I'm with you. If only I could risk telling you, but I can't because you'd run a mile.*

Instead, she spoke brightly, sounding confident. 'All right, I'm sensible and I know what I'm doing, so you listen and take my advice.'

'Yes, ma'am.'

'Stretch your arm a little way across the table so that your hand's close to mine, but not touching.'

He did so.

'Inch your fingers just a little bit further.'

'As though I was longing to touch you but didn't dare,' he suggested.

'That's right. You've got the idea.'

He did it perfectly, fingers almost brushing hers, drawing back quickly, then venturing forth again. She wondered how often he'd done this for real, teasing a girl into thinking that he was her humble suppliant, and involuntarily gave a small choke of laughter.

'What's so funny?' he asked. 'Aren't I doing it right?'

'Perfectly. In fact, too perfectly. This is how you get the girls to like you, isn't it? Make them think you're meek and hesitant, and they're in control.'

'You *are* in control,' he pointed out.

'But you're not trying to win my heart. I mean the others. I'll bet it works with them.'

He grinned. 'Sometimes. Some like it that way, some like a man to seem more dominant. I have to vary it.'

'You're a cheeky so-and-so,' she said.

'That's another approach that pays dividends,' he admitted. 'All right, all right, I know we're only play-acting. I'm not aiming to win dividends from you, I promise. I wouldn't dare.'

'Just don't forget that,' she said, trying to sound stern.

At the same moment they both burst out laughing. Heads turned at the sight of Mark Sellon having such a good time with Sylvia's sister, then nodded wisely. Aha! Perhaps that was the reason Sylvia had vanished.

'Permission to touch your fingers,' Mark murmured.

'Just a little.'

His fingertips brushed hers, withdrew, advanced again, paused, withdrew.

'Don't overdo the meek bit,' she advised.

'I'm nervous. I fear your rejection.'

She choked again. 'Stop it,' she said in a quivering voice. 'I can't keep a straight face. You don't do "nervous" very convincingly. It doesn't come naturally to you.'

For answer, he took her hand in his, letting them lie together on the table.

'Thank you,' he said. 'I feel happier holding your hand. I'm not sure I could cope without you. I'm just so confused by all this—'

His grip tightened suddenly. Dee didn't speak, but grasped him in return, knowing it was the only comfort that would get through to him now. He smiled and nodded to say he understood, and they stayed like that in silence until he said, 'Let's go. Getting drunk doesn't seem like such a good idea any more.'

Hand in hand, they rose and headed for the door.

'They're watching us,' she murmured.

'Then let's give them something to watch,' he said, pulling her close and laying his mouth on hers.

It was gentle, not passionate; a kiss for show, with just enough there to tell the onlookers what they wanted to know, then it was over and he escorted her out.

'You didn't mind my doing that?' he asked as they walked away.

'No, it was very clever,' she assured him breathlessly. 'Just what we needed to finish the show.' With an effort, she assumed a comically lofty tone. 'I thought we did that rather well.'

'So do I. In fact, I think I can hear applause.'

As one, they stopped and took elaborate bows to an unseen audience. People walking in the street hurried to the other side, well away from this alarming pair.

'You see that?' she said. 'They think we're mad.'

'How could anybody think that?' he demanded dramatically.

'Anyone who knows us, I imagine.'

He tightened his arm around her, not to kiss her now, but to lean sideways and let his cheek rest against her hair.

'Yes, they don't know the half of it,' he agreed.

'But at least we're mad together. We have that.'

'It's the only thing that's keeping me sane right now.'

At her doorway, he stopped, saying, 'Let me take you out somewhere tomorrow night.'

'Yes, we must be convincing.'

'No, that's not the reason. I want to thank you for everything you're doing. I don't know how you put up with me.'

'I work hard at it.'

'Good. Don't stop. Tomorrow night, then.'

'Actually, I can't,' she said with dismay. 'I'm working tomorrow night, and every night until the end of this week.'

'You're not trying to dump me already, are you? At least it took Sylvia four months to get fed up with me.'

'Don't be daft,' she chuckled. 'I'm on duty at the hospital. I'm a working woman.'

'Then I'll wait on your pleasure. Let me know the first night you can manage.'

He hesitated, and for a blissful moment she thought he would kiss her. And he did. But only on the tip of her nose. Then he walked away, fast.

Dee entered the house quietly, hoping that her parents would have gone to bed, but they were still up. To her relief, they greeted her calmly and Helen had softened towards Mark.

'I was a bit hard on him, wasn't I? It's not his fault. Is he all right?'

'He's coping. I'm trying to help him,' Dee said. 'But he needs time. I'm going to bed now. Goodnight.'

She hurried away, unable to endure any more talking. She

wanted to be alone with her memories of the evening. Mark's heart was still Sylvia's, and she knew she was a long way from the fulfilment of her dream. But for a while she'd had him to herself, enjoyed his whole attention, felt his lips on hers.

In bed she snuggled down, pulling the blankets over her head so that the world was reduced to this tiny space where she could relive his kiss again and again, and dream of the time when it would be truly meant for her.

'One day,' she whispered. 'One day soon—please—'

She was young enough to believe that if she desired something fiercely enough she could make it happen. Wasn't he already half hers? It was just a question of being patient. She was smiling as she fell asleep.

For the next few days she saw him only briefly as he arrived for work in the garage. Her hours were full as her duties increased. Although still technically a student, she was at the top of her class and often assigned to extra duties around the hospital. These were always carried out under the eagle-eye of her superiors, but she was trusted more than any of the others, due to Mr Royce's recommendation. He seldom praised her to her face. But she came to realise that he expressed a high opinion of her to others.

When she tried to thank him, he was polite but reserved.

'You must all become the best nurses in the world,' he said, 'because you'll soon be needed.'

'You really believe there'll be a war?'

'Certainly I do. And so does every thinking person. Now get to work and pass those exams in style.'

From Sylvia there was no word, but one evening, as she was leaving for work, she found a letter for her at the reception desk. It had been delivered by hand.

I dare not write to you at home, in case Mum finds the letter first and tears it up. I know Mum will say I'm a disgrace to the family, and Dad will agree with her because he always does. But perhaps I can explain to you, make you understand.

You're wondering how I could ever have left Mark, aren't you? You see, I know how you feel about him. It was there in your eyes when you weren't guarding them.

I did once think I was in love with him. Any girl would feel that. He's good-looking, charming and fun. They were all after him and I felt proud that he'd chosen me. But then things went wrong. He seemed to feel that he had the right to do as he liked and never mind anyone else. He didn't mean to be selfish but he's made that way. If he wanted to flirt, he flirted. If I showed that I minded, I was 'making a fuss about nothing'.

On New Year's Eve, when you saw me fooling around with other lads, I was only trying to make Mark jealous. Even back then he was too sure of me. I thought it wouldn't hurt him to know he's not the only man in the world, but it didn't really work because he's so self-confident.

Do you remember that talk we had one night, when I said that there were other men who wanted me? I think I already knew that Phil was the one. I know he's married, and it's wrong. I'm a 'bad girl'. But he's kind and gentle, and he loves me. He tries to please me because it matters to him that I'm happy. Mark never cared in that way.

There was one final paragraph that stood out starkly.

Be careful, my dear. Don't let Mark hurt you, which he could do very easily. I was lucky. I saw through him, but you might not. Love him a little, if you must, but don't give him your whole heart. He won't know what to do with it.

Dee couldn't read any more. Inside her was a storm of confused feelings. Selfish. Inconsiderate. Self-centred. That was how Sylvia saw Mark, and it wasn't true. How could she say such things? *They weren't true!*

Then the real reason came to her. Sylvia was simply trying to justify herself at Mark's expense. The relief was enormous. Of course he wasn't anything like that.

But you were, my darling. In some ways, you were like two men. One was the man who behaved so generously over the ruined bike, and was so tender and kind to Billy.

The other man was exactly as Sylvia had described. And why not? You were twenty-three and far too handsome for your own good, never mind anyone else's. You looked like a film star, people treated you like a film star, and so you acted like a film star. It's amazing that you were as kind and sweet-tempered as you were.

I didn't see it, of course. These days, a girl of eighteen can be sophisticated, but in those days you were still practically a child, under your parents' authority. I was far too immature myself to recognise immaturity in you, or I might have noticed that Sylvia's actions hurt your pride more than your heart. I thought you were perfect, and I tried to forget what she'd said about you.

But I couldn't. Now and then there'd be a moment when I saw what she'd been talking about, despite how much I loved you.

Why are you sleeping so restlessly? Are you having those troubled dreams again? You haven't had them for years, but I suppose the party tonight brought it all back. There, there! Let me make it better, like I did before. You always said there was no one like me to help you fight the nightmares.

Hush, my darling! I'm here...I'm here.

CHAPTER SIX

ONE night in March, when Mark was to take her out for supper, she arrived home from work, expecting to find him.

'He's not here,' her father said. 'I had to give him the day off.'

'But where has he gone?'

'I don't know. He wouldn't say. Very mysterious, he was. But he wants you to meet him at that new café down the road, and he says you're to wear your best dress.'

On winged feet she flew down the street, bursting into the café and looking around for him eagerly.

He wasn't there.

Never mind. Soon. Just be patient. She ordered a pot of tea and settled down to wait and plan. Between work and studying her schedule was heavy, but still she could count on an outing with him once a week, to maintain their pretence. And she would use that time to win his heart, so that gradually she would become his real girlfriend and then…perhaps…

Be sensible. You're not a lovelorn dreamer. You're Nurse Parsons, top of the class, probably Matron Parsons one day.

But who wanted to be sensible? With a little female cunning, it could all be made to happen just as she wanted. She began to feel like the scheming, adventurous women of history. Messalina, Delilah, Cleopatra; they had nothing on her. Soon Mark would sigh at her feet.

Or at least he might if he were here.

She had to wait an hour for him, but her heart soared when she saw his expression. He was lit up, brilliant with excitement. He rushed over, planted a kiss on her mouth, then settled in the seat opposite, holding her hands in his and almost shaking them in his eagerness.

She could have wept with joy to think that a meeting with her could do this to him.

'I can't tell you—' he said, almost stammering. 'If you only knew—all the way here I've been thinking what to say—'

'To say what?' she begged, inwardly singing.

'I've done it at last. It came over me suddenly that this was the perfect time. I lay awake all last night planning it, and this morning I asked your father for the day off.' He took a deep breath. 'I've done it. I've joined up.'

'You've—what?'

'I've joined the Air Force. Not the official force but the Auxiliaries.'

She knew what he meant because since the time he'd first mentioned his desire to fly, she'd done some reading on the subject. The Auxiliary Air Force was a corps of civilians who learned flying skills and were ready to be called up if war broke out.

'I'll stay here,' Mark said, 'but go for training at weekends. When the war begins, I'll become part of the official force.'

'When it begins? Not if?'

'Come on, we all know what's going to happen. They're about to start conscripting men of my age, and if I'd left it any longer I could have been drafted into the army. By acting now, I've made sure I choose the service I want to join. And it means I can learn to fly. Isn't that wonderful?'

'Wonderful,' she echoed.

And that was it. The dream of winning his love, his joyful look that she'd thought was for her—what had she been thinking of? He barely knew she existed.

Stupid, stupid girl! Sit here and listen to him, try to sound enthusiastic, don't let him guess what you're really feeling.

'It'll be easier on you, too,' he said. 'I won't be around so much so you won't have to pretend to be my girlfriend nearly as often. We'll just make an appearance now and then.'

'That's very thoughtful of you,' she said faintly.

Sylvia seemed to be there whispering, *Be careful. He's not thinking of you really. He's done what* he *wants.*

'You said once that you dreamed of flying,' she mused.

'Someone told me you had to have the "right background" before the Auxiliaries would look at you. But they're taking in more people now because they know what's coming. And I'm going to be part of it. I'm going to be a pilot, maybe fly a Spitfire or a Hurricane, and it'll be the best thing that ever happened to me.'

'Unless you get killed,' she murmured.

'I won't get killed. I'm indestructible.'

'But you're getting ready to fight. You could be shot down, or just crash.'

'Why are you being so gloomy?' he asked, faintly irritated. 'I've got my heart's desire and you can only look on the dark side.'

'Well, if you got hurt or killed I would find that rather gloomy,' she said, troubled by his inability to understand.

'That's very nice of you, but let's not dwell on something that isn't going to happen. Come on, let's get out of here and celebrate.'

'Is this why I'm in my best dress?'

'Yes, we're going to The Star Barn, that dance hall in Cavey Street.'

In a plush dance hall the music came from an orchestra. The poorer ones had a piano or gramophone records. The Star Barn compromised with a three-piece band that made up in volume what it lacked in skill.

She was still a little hurt at the way Mark seemed absorbed

in his own point of view and oblivious to hers. It came too close to Sylvia's warning. But the feeling vanished as he took her into his arms, and she felt the vivid joy that possessed him communicate itself to her flesh from his. Impossible to stay troubled while her body was against his, their faces so close, his eyes alight with an almost demonic energy.

One dance ran into another until the whole evening was an endless stream of movement. It had been a hard day at work and she'd been tired at the start of the evening, but mysteriously she wasn't tired now. Every moment with him invigorated her.

'You're a terrific dancer,' he said, gasping slightly. 'Let's go faster.'

'Yes, let's.'

She managed to seize the initiative, driving him on until they were both breathless, and somehow they danced out of the hall into the deserted lobby. To the end of her days she had no memory of how they'd got there.

'You shouldn't have done that,' Mark warned her.

'Why?'

'Because now I'm going to do this,' he said, taking her in his arms and kissing her firmly.

It wasn't like the other times, a skilful pretence to deceive onlookers. They were alone and it was the real thing. Now the pressure of his mouth was intense and determined, saying that he wasn't fooling any more and what was she going to do about it?

There was only one possible answer. It was she who moved her lips first, not to escape his but to caress them, revel in the sensation and drive him on further. It was something she'd never done before and she didn't understand how she knew about it. The knowledge seemed to have been part of her for ever, dormant, waiting for this moment to awake. Now it wasn't merely awake but triumphant, determined to make the most of every last thrilling moment.

She was a novice, exploring the first steps of physical love, learning fast but needing to learn more. He taught her, moving his mouth against hers with practised skill, teasing, inciting, leading her blissfully to the next lesson, and then the next. She pressed closer, every inch of her clamouring to learn.

Then, with cruel abruptness, it was over and he was pushing her away from him. When she tried to reach for him again he fended her off.

'Stop it, Dee. *We have to stop!*' His voice was harsh, almost cruel.

'I'm sorry…what—? Did I do something wrong?' She was almost in tears.

'No, you did everything right—too right. That's the problem.'

She misunderstood and her hands flew to her mouth. 'You think I'm a bad girl, that I always do this, but you're wrong, you're wrong.'

'No, I don't mean that. I know you're innocent. You must be or you'd have been more careful. Only an innocent would have pushed me to the edge like that.'

'I don't understand,' she whispered.

He sighed. 'No, you don't, do you?' He took her back into his arms, but pressing her head against his shoulder, careful to avoid her face. 'Don't cry. It's not your fault. But I had to stop when I did, or I wouldn't have been able to stop at all, and then I'd have done something that would make you hate me.'

She couldn't answer. Her heart was thundering, her whole body trembling with thwarted desire.

Hate him? What did he mean? She hated him now for leaving her like this, desperate to go on to the end and discover the secret. She pressed closer to him, hoping to remind him of what they had shared, what they might still share.

'Let's go home,' he said grimly.

They went home in silence. He didn't even hold her hand,

but kept several feet away. Dee crossed her arms over her chest as though trying to protect herself and walked with her head down, staring at the pavement, feeling alienated from the whole world, but especially from the man she loved, who was acting as though she didn't exist.

When they stopped at her front door he seemed uneasy and there was a thoughtful look on his face.

'You're full of surprises,' he said. 'I guess there's a lot more to you than meets the eye. Don't look at me like that. I can't explain right now, especially as your mother is just behind the curtains, watching us. But you…well, anyway…'

He dropped a modest peck on her cheek, said a hurried, 'Goodnight,' and walked away.

Weary and depressed, Dee let herself into the house. As Mark had observed, Helen was waiting for her, in dressing gown and curlers.

'Well?' she demanded. 'Did he behave himself?'

'Oh, yes,' Dee said softly. 'He behaved himself. Goodnight, Mum.'

She ran upstairs as fast as she could.

As Mark had predicted, conscription started the following month, and he'd been wise to get into the Air Force while he still had a choice.

Now she saw him only briefly, as his free time was taken up by the squadron, located just outside London. Joe was immensely proud of him and showed it by giving him Saturdays off so that he could devote the whole weekend to training to be a pilot.

'I couldn't be more proud if he was my own son,' he confided to his wife. 'And, after all, that may happen.' He finished with a significant look at Dee, out in the garden.

'Hmm!' Helen said. 'Hasn't he caused enough trouble in this family?'

'It wasn't his fault; I thought we agreed that.'

'I just don't like what's happening to Dee. Something's not right.'

'She's just missing him. It's happening all over the country now the men are joining up.'

He began inviting Mark in for supper on the days he knew Dee would be home, partly for his daughter's sake and partly because he was consumed with curiosity. He loved nothing better than to listen while Mark described his life as a budding pilot.

'They let me take the controls the other day,' he recalled once. 'I can't begin to tell you what it's like up there, feeling as though all the power in the world was yours, and you could do anything you wanted.'

'I remember when the war started in nineteen fourteen,' Joe said. 'Nobody thought of using planes to fight; they were so frail, just bits of wood and canvas. But then someone mounted a machine gun and that was that. Next thing, we had a Royal Air Force. I'd have loved to fly, but blokes like me just got stuck in the trenches.'

They became more absorbed in their conversation, while Dee's eyes met her mother's across the table in a silent message. *Men!*

'There's something I have to tell you,' Mark said at last. 'They've put my name down for a new course. I'm the first in my group to be assigned to it—'

'Good for you,' Joe said. 'They know you're the best. But it means you'll spend more time there and less here, doesn't it?'

'I'm afraid so. They reckon the war will be declared pretty soon, so then I'll be in the Air Force full-time. Perhaps you should start looking for another mechanic.'

Dee heard all this from a distance. It was coming, the thing she dreaded, the moment when he would walk away to the war and she might never see him again. Time was rushing by.

She had grown cautious, sensing a slight change in Mark's

manner. Since the night she'd come alive in his arms, she'd sometimes caught him giving her a curious look. She was shocked at herself, wondering if her forward behaviour had damaged his respect for her.

When they were alone, his kisses were fervent, even passionate, as though he was discovering something new about her all the time. But then he would draw back as though he'd thought better of it, leaving her in a state of confusion. With all her heart she longed to take him past that invisible barrier, and she hadn't much time left to make it happen.

After supper the three of them listened to the wireless. The official news from Europe was worrying, but what had really caught people's attention was the fact that when King George VI and Queen Elizabeth went on a visit to Canada, they were escorted by two warships.

'And there's a rumour that those ships carried thirty million pounds in gold, for safe-keeping in Canada until it's all over,' Mark had said.

Until it was all over. What would life be like then? Another universe in which he might, or might not be alive. She shivered.

She tried to speak normally, but it was hard when everything in her was focused on one thing—to be alone with Mark, in his arms, kissing him and being kissed, feeling her body burn with new life. Her heart was breaking, yet she must try to pretend all was well.

At last he rose. 'I think I'll take a breath of fresh air,' he said casually.

Eagerly, she joined him and they slipped out into the privacy of the garden. The next moment she was in his arms.

'Why must you go now?' she begged. 'It's too soon.'

'I have to. But I'm going to miss you so much,' he said hoarsely.

'Yes…yes…'

The thought of the lonely time without him lent urgency

to her movements. In the past she'd fought down the blazing desire that almost overcame her when she was in his arms, but tonight she didn't want to be controlled and virtuous. She wanted to let herself go and risk whatever the future held. If that meant being a 'bad girl', then so be it, as long as she could say that just once he'd been hers.

He lifted his head and his eyes and his breathing told her that he was in the same state. Another moment and they would become each other's and who cared for anything else?

'Mark,' she whispered, '*Mark*—'

'Do you want me?'

'*Yes*—'

Urgently, he drew her down onto the grass and she gave herself up to the feel of his lips on her neck, drifting lower as he opened the buttons of her blouse. High above, the spring moon beamed down on her like a blessing, and she prepared herself for what would surely be the most beautiful experience of her life.

Transported, she didn't hear the door opening behind them, only her mother's voice coming out of nowhere in an outraged cry of, '*You can stop that!*'

She felt Mark freeze on top of her, heard his muttered curse. Then he drew away, helping her to her feet.

'Mum,' she said desperately, 'it's not—'

'Don't you try to fool me, my girl. I know what it's not, and I know what it *is*. It's shameful, that's what it is. I thought you were a good girl, with more self-respect.'

'Come on, Helen,' her husband begged under his voice. 'After all, didn't we—?'

'You hush.' She turned on him furiously.

'Yes, dear.'

'You—' she turned on Mark '—you should be ashamed of yourself, acting like that in a decent home. Just what do you think my daughter is?'

'Well, I was hoping she'd become my wife,' Mark replied.

Slowly, Dee turned her head towards him as the world exploded about her, full of blazing light and riotous colours. It had happened. He'd proposed. She would be his wife. Every dream had come true. Passionate joy held her speechless.

Helen, too, was briefly dumb, but she was the first to recover. 'That puts a different face on it,' she said, cautious and not entirely yielding. 'If you mean it.'

'I was going to ask Dee tonight, only you interrupted me.'

Joe began to edge his wife away. 'Goodnight, you two,' he said with a touch of desperation as he managed to get Helen inside.

Dee's head was clearing and her sensible side reasserting itself, as it had a terrible habit of doing. She'd be a fool to believe this.

'It's all right, Mark,' she said in a low voice. 'You don't have to marry me.'

He regarded her, his head on one side. 'Maybe I want to. Have you thought of that?'

'You don't want to. You just had to divert my mother. I understand.'

'Now you've insulted me,' he said cheerfully.

'Have I?'

'There I am, learning to take to the skies and fight Hitler, and you think I'm afraid of your mother. She's formidable, I grant you, but I'm not scared of her.'

She gave a shaky laugh. 'I didn't mean that, but you know as well as I do that you weren't going to propose if we hadn't got caught.'

'Well, perhaps she did us a favour by showing us the way. Are you saying you don't want to marry me?'

'It's not that, it's just—'

He put his hands on her shoulders and spoke lightly. 'My

darling, will you give a straight answer to a straight question? Are you turning me down?'

'No, of course not, I—'

'Then are you accepting me?'

She looked up into his face, trying to read the truth behind his quizzical expression. She saw humour and good nature, but not the answer she needed.

'Yes or no?' he persisted.

'Yes,' she said with a kind of desperation. It wasn't the proposal she'd dreamed of, and in her heart she knew something about it wasn't right, but there was no way she could turn down the chance to make him hers.

'Does that mean we're engaged?'

'Yes,' she choked. *'Oh, yes!'*

This time their kiss was relatively restrained, since both knew that Helen was watching them from the kitchen window. As they returned slowly to the house, she was waiting for them. Joe produced drinks to celebrate, then Helen declared that it was late and Mark would be wanting to get home. She wore a fixed smile but both her expression and her tone said, *No hanky-panky in this house.*

Mark gave Dee a rueful smile and departed under the steely gaze of his future mother-in-law.

'Congratulations, love,' Joe said, embracing his daughter.

'Yes, you got him to the finishing post,' Helen agreed, although she couldn't resist adding, 'with a bit of help.'

'Mum!'

'He'd have taken his time proposing if I hadn't prodded him on. Never mind. We managed it. We should be proud of ourselves.'

'But that's not how it's supposed to happen,' Dee protested.

'The important thing is, it happened. You wouldn't want him going off to the Air Force without having his ring on your finger. He wasn't going to propose, just fool around with you and then on to the next. Look what he did to Sylvia.'

'Look what she did to him,' Dee said quickly.

'Does she still write to you, love?' Joe asked gently. She had told them about the first letter and read out some, but not all of its contents.

'Now and then. Doesn't she ever write to you?'

'She's tried,' Helen said. 'I tear them up.'

'Before I even see them,' Joe said sadly. 'We don't even know where she is.'

'She hasn't told me her address,' Dee said. 'But she's living with Phil and in her last letter she said she'd just discovered that she was pregnant.'

Helen stiffened. 'So as well as being a whore, she's going to have a little bastard. I want nothing to do with her. Anyway, at least we'll have one respectable marriage in this family. Get him tied to you while you can, my girl. I've done my best for you. Now it's up to you.'

If she'd thought to encourage Dee into marriage by this means, she was mistaken. Whatever Mark said, she couldn't rid herself of the shamed feeling that he'd simply taken the line of least resistance. One part of her mind urged her to rush the ceremony before he could back off, but the other part refused to do it.

These days the world seemed to be thrown into sharp relief, and everything had a sense of 'one last time before the war'. Any party or celebration, every anniversary, any piece of good fortune, must be enjoyed to the full. Just in case.

'There's a fair on Hampstead Heath,' Mark told her one evening. 'Let's go. We never know when there'll be another one.'

The Heath was a magical place, a great green park barely four miles from the centre of London. It had always been a popular venue for fairs, and especially now as the dark days approached.

As they neared the fair, they could hear the unmistakable sound of the hurdy-gurdy blaring over the distance. From far off, the giant wheel glittered as it turned against the night.

'I've always wanted to go up on one of those,' she breathed.

'We will, I promise.'

Close up, the wheel was even more dazzling.

'Ever been on one?' Mark asked.

'No. I've often wanted to, but I was always at the fair with my parents and Mum said, "You don't want to go on those dangerous things". And I didn't know how to tell her that I did want to *because* they were dangerous.'

'Right,' he said. 'Come on.' He bought the tickets and took her hand firmly. 'Those seats rock back and forth like mad, so hold onto me.'

From the moment they sat down and she felt the seat swinging beneath her, Dee felt as though she'd come home. Nothing in her life had ever been as exciting as when she was lifted high into the air, over the top of the wheel, then the descent when, for a moment, there seemed to be nothing but air between herself and the earth beneath. Then again, and again, loving it more every moment.

'Wheeeee!' she shrieked as they arrived back at the bottom for the final time. 'I want to go again.'

He took her up three times, finally saying, 'Leave it for now. There are other rides, just as exciting.'

'Lead me to them!'

Her eyes were gleaming as they approached the roller coaster, and she looked up the climb with an eagerness that anticipated the pleasure to come. She could just see a car reaching the summit and hear the shrieks as it sped down.

'Come *on!*' she begged.

He looked at her curiously. 'Aren't you afraid?'

'What of?' she asked blankly.

'You'll find out,' he said, grinning.

When they were seated he made as if to put an arm around her. 'But perhaps you're too brave to need my help?' he teased.

'I don't think I'm quite as brave as that,' she conceded, pulling his arm about her shoulders.

The cars moved off, slowly at first, climbing the long slope to the summit, then plunging down at ever increasing speed while she screamed with pleasure and huddled closer to him.

After two more rides he insisted that they get out, at least for a while.

'You may not need a rest, but I do,' he gasped. 'Where's the beer tent?'

In the tent, they sat down and sipped light ale. Every nerve throughout her body was singing with excitement, but the greatest pleasure was the look Mark was giving her, as though seeing her for the first time and admiring what he saw.

'I never guessed you enjoyed that kind of thing,' he said.

'Neither did I. If I'd known, I'd have done it sooner.'

'Most girls don't care for it,' he said, speaking more quietly than was usual with him.

And suddenly Sylvia was there with them, gasping and clinging to them in horror after her ride in the sidecar, vowing *never again*.

'I'm not most girls,' Dee said brightly. 'I'm mad. Hadn't you heard?'

'If I hadn't, I know now.'

She drained her glass and held it out. 'Can I have another one?'

'No,' he said in alarm. 'Your mother would kill me. She already disapproves of me, even though we're engaged.'

Dee nodded. Helen wanted them married for the sake of respectability, but only that morning she'd said, 'I know he can talk the hind legs off a donkey and he's got a cheeky smile, but you mark my words. He's a bad boy!'

Which was true, Dee thought. Mark's 'bad boy' aspect was seldom on display, but it was always there, just below the surface. It lived in uneasy partnership with his generous side and it made him thrilling. But she wouldn't have dared to tell her mother that. She didn't fully understand it herself. She only knew that he lived in her heart as the most exciting man in the world and she wouldn't have him any different.

CHAPTER SEVEN

WHEN they came to the dodgems she insisted on their taking a car each so that they could bash each other. Once behind the wheel, she laid into him with a will. But he gave as good as he got and when they joined up again afterwards they agreed that honours were even.

But in one thing he beat her hollow—on the rifle range his aim was perfect. He scored bullseyes with ease and was offered his pick of the prizes on display. He chose a small fluffy teddy bear and solemnly presented it to her.

She fell in love with it at once. The face was slightly lop-sided, giving it an air of cheeky humour that she instantly recognised.

'He's you,' she said.

'Me?' he asked, startled.

'Well, he's rather better-looking than you, of course,' she said, considering. 'But that cocky air is exactly you. My bruin.'

'Bruin?'

'It's an old word for bear. This isn't just an ordinary bear. He's *my* bear. He's a real bruin.' She dropped a kiss on the furry little fellow's snout.

'I'm jealous,' Mark said.

'How can you be jealous of yourself?' she demanded, tucking the toy safely into her bag.

'I'll think about that.'

He bought two ice creams and they wandered through the fair, hand in hand. Dee thought she'd never known such a happy evening.

'Will you take me on the roller coaster again?' she asked.

'Am I allowed to say no?'

'Not a chance.'

Suddenly a yell came out of the darkness.

'Look at that!' someone breathed, pointing upward, horrified and admiring at the same time.

High above them stretched what looked like a hollow pole made of metal latticework. A string of lights went up the middle, gleaming against the metal strips and illuminating the man who was climbing to the top.

'He shouldn't be doing that!'

'He's crazy!'

'Yes, but what a climber!'

The shouts filled the air, but the climbing man seemed oblivious to the sensation he was creating. Up, up he moved, never looking down, untroubled by the height, although the pole was beginning to sway.

'Is he going right to the top?'

'He won't dare. It isn't safe.'

It seemed that the man agreed, because he stopped and made a dramatic gesture to the crowd below, signifying the end of the performance. Cheers erupted as he began to descend and applause filled the air.

'What's that for?' Mark demanded indignantly. 'He got nowhere near the top.'

'He got pretty high, though,' Dee pointed out.

'Anybody can settle for second best. It's reaching the top that matters.'

'Yes, if you want to risk your neck for nothing,' she said.

As soon as the words were out she knew they were a mistake and the look on Mark's face confirmed it. To him, the risk alone was worth it. The more danger, the more fun; those had been his words.

'Mark—wait!' she cried as he turned away, resolution written in every line of his body.

He ignored her, if he even heard her. Terrified now, she seized his arm and at last he turned.

'Take your hands off me,' he said softly.

'Mark, please—'

'Let go, *now!*'

She'd never heard such a tone from him before, or seen such a look in his eyes. Where was the sweet-tempered joker that she loved? Gone, and in his place this hard-faced man who would brook no interference in his wishes.

'I told you to let me go,' he repeated coldly.

Appalled, she stepped back, her hands falling away from him as the strength drained out of them.

He was a stranger, a man she'd never met before and never wanted to meet again. In her heart she'd always known something like this was waiting for them, a moment when she would look down the road ahead and shiver.

Mark saw her withdrawn expression and misunderstood it.

'It's all right,' he said, speaking more gently. 'I know what I'm doing.'

He was gone before she could reply, striding towards the terrifying pole, leaping onto the bottom rung and climbing fast before anyone could stop him. Now there were more cheers, mingled with screams.

Dee's heart almost stopped. It was unbearable to watch him, yet impossible to look away. He was approaching the point where the first man had given up. If only he would be satisfied with going a little further and claiming victory! Surely that would be enough for him!

'Please, please,' she whispered. 'Make him stop—let him be satisfied without going to the top.'

But he wouldn't be satisfied with less, she knew that. It had to be all or nothing. That was how he was made.

The crowd roared as he reached the crucial point and climbed beyond it. On the ground, the other climber groaned and swore. 'Show-off,' he growled.

'And what were you?' Dee turned on him.

'All right, I'm a show-off too, but I knew when to stop. The metal's much thinner up there. It won't support him.'

Right on cue, a metal strut bent under Mark's foot. He hesitated, clinging on, looking down, then looking up.

'Come down,' yelled someone. 'Be sensible.'

Fatal. Be sensible! Like a red rag to a bull, Dee thought frantically.

At last he tightened his grip, raised his head to the sky and began to climb again. The pole swayed but this time the crowd didn't scream. Instead, there was silence, as though the universe had stopped until they knew what would happen.

Four more rungs, then three—two—one—and finally—

The roar was deafening as Mark reached the summit and threw up one arm in victory, waving down at them as the applause streamed up to him in waves.

'*Did you see that?*'

'*What a hero that man must be!*'

'*He's not afraid of anything.*'

Gradually he descended while everyone in the crowd crossed their fingers, willing him to succeed, until at last he vanished into their open arms and the roar exploded again.

'Hey, aren't you with him?'

Dee opened her eyes to see a young couple.

'We saw you talking,' the boy said. 'Are you his girl-friend?'

'I…er…yes.'

'You must be so proud of him,' the girl sighed. To her companion she said, 'You never do things like that.'

'Then you're very lucky,' Dee said with a tartness that even took herself by surprise and moved away quickly.

Mark saw her coming and threw up his arms, his eyes alight. Everything in his manner said, *How about that?*

'Are you all right?' she asked.

'Of course I'm all right. It was nothing.'

'It was reckless and stupid,' said a man who'd appeared behind him. He was middle-aged and heavily built. 'I'm the owner of this fair and I've a good mind to hand you over to the police for damage to my property.'

There were cries of indignation. 'You can't do that—we're gonna need fellows like him soon—'

'I didn't say I was going to,' the owner defended himself. 'I've never seen anything like it.' He shook Mark's hand. 'Just don't do it again.'

Roars of laughter. More applause. Congratulations. Dee watched, wondering why she couldn't join in the general delight, but she didn't want to spoil it for him so she tried to smile brightly as she approached, playing the role of the woman proud to bursting point of her man.

Clearly it was what he was expecting, for he flung his arms around her and drew her close in an exuberant embrace. The crowd loved that, clapping their hands, laughing and hooting.

She never heard them. The feel of his lips on hers almost deprived her of her senses. It wasn't the kiss she longed for, intimate, loving, personal. It was a kiss for show, but it was the best she could hope for and she would relish every moment. She kissed him back, putting her heart into it, wondering if he could ever recognise that she even had a heart.

The crowd's applause brought her back down to earth. Embarrassed, she drew back and began to walk away.

'You're very quiet,' he said as he caught up with her. 'Are you annoyed with me?'

'You're an idiot!' she told him.

'No question!' He rested his hands on her shoulders. 'I know I'm a fool, but you'll forgive me, won't you? It's just me, it's the way I am. Once a fool, always a fool.'

She pulled the toy bear out of her bag and held him up so that they could look at each other, face to face.

'You hear that?' she said. 'He admitted he's a fool. I suppose you're on his side. Mad bruins, both of you.'

He chuckled. 'Mad Bruin. I like it.'

She knew a little flare of anger at his lack of understanding. She'd suffered a thousand agonies watching him, but that had never occurred to him. He'd seen only what he wanted to do and the satisfaction it gave him. Now he was up in the clouds, bursting with delight, and no thought for her.

But then, she thought, why should he think of her? He didn't know that she was in love with him. It probably hadn't occurred to him that she suffered.

Stop complaining, she told herself. You chose to become engaged to a man who's not in love with you. Live with it!

'Wait here,' she said, rising suddenly and darting away.

In a few moments she was back at the stall where he'd won the little bear.

'He's lonely,' she said, holding Bruin up. 'He wants his mate. How much to buy her?'

'You're supposed to win her,' the stall-holder protested.

'With my aim, we'll be here all night. How much?'

He haggled briefly but gave in and sold her the little toy, identical to the other except for a frilly skirt. Then she raced back to Mark and thrust her trophy into his hand.

'There you are! Now we both have one.'

'You won this? I'm impressed.'

Briefly she was torn by temptation, but wisdom prevailed. 'No, I persuaded him to sell her to me.'

'How much?'

She grimaced. 'One shilling and sixpence.'

'*How much?* That's a fortune. You could buy several pints of beer for that.'

'I buy only the best,' she assured him. 'This is female Bruin, and she's going to keep an eye on you for me.'

'Going to nag me, eh?'

'Definitely. And spy on you, and report back to me if you get up to mischief.' But then she added in a quieter voice, 'And look after you.'

'Stop me doing stupid things?'

'Something like that.'

'Then I'd better look after her,' he said. He made as if to tuck the toy into his jacket but held her up at the last minute.

'She says it's getting late and we ought to go home,' he said.

'And she's always right.'

Hand in hand, they strolled out of the fair.

She remembered that evening long afterwards, for it was the last one of its kind. Soon after that, the lights of London went out one night, leaving the city in darkness and people groping their way home.

'It's only a trial,' Joe reassured them, holding up a candle. 'When the war starts, London will have to be blacked out for its own safety every night. This is to warn us to get ready.'

Sure enough, the lights eventually returned, but the sudden darkness had brought the truth home as nothing else could have done. Now it was real. Mark was no longer an Auxiliary but a part of the official Air Force, his skills honed to a fine edge, waiting for the formal declaration of war, and at last it came.

Now nothing would ever be the same again.

Mark managed a brief visit. Helen treated him as an honoured guest, preparing a special supper and leaving Dee only a few moments alone with him before he had to leave for the airfield where he would always be on call. As she watched him walk away, she wondered when or if she would see him again.

All around her the world was changing. Children were evacuated out of London to distant farms, men joined up or were conscripted, young women also joined up or went to work in factories or on farms, replacing the men. Dee briefly considered joining the Women's Auxiliary Air Force, an ambition that Mr Royce crushed without hesitation.

'You're a nurse—or you will be when you've passed your exams, very soon. I expect you to do well, and you'll be far more use to your country exercising your medical skills.'

It was the closest anyone had heard him come to a compliment.

By now, everyone knew that war would be declared any day, and when it finally happened on 3rd September there was almost a sense of relief in the air. Now they could get on with things. Some of the patients even cheered.

Dee kept smiling, but when she was alone she slipped away into the hospital chapel and sat there, thinking of Mark, wondering what the future held.

Her exams came and went. Later, she could barely remember taking them, but she passed well and was offered a permanent job at the hospital.

Congratulations abounded. Matron told her she'd always known it would happen. Mr Royce, no longer a distant figure of authority, approached her in the canteen and insisted on buying her a cup of tea 'to celebrate'.

Mark managed to make it back for a small family celebration, but most of the day was spent building the Anderson shelter. These shelters were made of sheets of corrugated iron, bolted together at the top, with steel plates at either end. They were set up in the garden, sunk as far as possible in the earth, for greater safety.

'I'm not sleeping in that thing,' Helen declared. 'We'll be better off in the house.'

'Not if they start to bomb this part of London,' Mark murmured.

He was reticent on the subject of his own sorties. Hitler was invading Europe, the British army had advanced in return and the Air Force was deployed to assist them. These bare facts were common knowledge, and beyond them he would say little.

The closest he came to revealing his feelings was as they were walking to the bus stop in the late afternoon. Nearby was a church, from which a couple was just emerging. The groom wore an army uniform. Instead of a wedding gown the bride wore a modest functional dress, only the flower on her shoulder suggesting that today was special.

'Is something the matter?' Mark asked, seeing her frown with concentration.

'No, I'm just trying to remember where I've seen her before. Ah, yes, she works in the bakery three streets away.'

The bride saw her and waved. Dee waved back.

'He's probably just home on leave for a few days and they won't have a honeymoon,' she reflected. 'There are so many of these quick weddings happening now.'

She didn't press it further, leaving it up to Mark whether he seized the point and pressed for a wedding of their own. He was silent for a moment and she crossed her fingers.

'Too many,' he said at last.

'What…what did you say?'

'There are too many of these mad weddings. He'll go away tomorrow and she may never see him again. If she does, he'll be changed, maybe disfigured.'

'But if she loved him she wouldn't be put off by his disfigurement.'

'She thinks she wouldn't. They all say that, but they don't know what they're talking about. The other day I met a man who was a pilot in the last war. His face had been destroyed by fire.'

Through her hand tucked under his arm, Dee felt the faint shudder that went through him.

'He hadn't seen his wife in years,' Mark continued. 'He didn't blame her. He said you couldn't expect a woman to endure looking at him day after day.'

'But he was still the same man inside,' Dee said, almost pleading.

'But he wasn't. How could he be? How could you face that fire and be the same inside?'

Again there was the shudder, stronger now, and her hand tightened in sympathy. These days she seemed to understand him better with every moment that passed, and she knew that he would die rather than admit to being afraid.

At first there had been no need to fear. Everything was beginning in sunlight and hope as the planes soared up and over Europe to tackle Hitler's invasion. But it soon became clear that the enemy had more powerful planes, and the British losses began to mount up. Mark was unscathed, but some of his friends weren't so lucky.

He hadn't told her, but she knew of two airmen whose bravery had resulted in the award of Victoria Crosses. But they never saw these tributes. They had died in action.

Now she had sensed the things that he could never put into words, and knew that secretly he dreaded fire more than anything else. More than pain. More than death. Fire.

'Maybe she won't be the same inside, either,' she said. 'Maybe she'll just be what he needs her to be.'

He gave a sharp, ironic laugh. 'If he's there at all. Suppose he dies and leaves her with a child to rear alone? Suppose she has no family left, and is really alone with a child she—is that the bus I can see in the distance?'

'Yes,' she said sadly.

'Time to go, then. Congratulations again on passing your

exams. I'll be in touch and we'll try to see each other again soon.'

The bus was there. An arm around her shoulder, a quick kiss on the mouth, and he was gone.

She didn't return home at once, but walked the streets as the light faded. Now she had her answer. There would be no early marriage, and perhaps no marriage at all. He'd expressed his refusal as consideration for her, and it sounded sensible enough, except that he didn't love her and needed a good excuse.

But then she remembered the echo from his own past, how he'd started to speak of the woman left alone with a child who she—and then he'd broken off. Who she—what? Couldn't cope with? Didn't love? What would he have said if the bus hadn't appeared at that moment? Would he tell her one day? Or would she be left to wonder all her life?

They managed a brief meeting over Christmas, but then time flashed by and it was 1940. As the months passed the prospect grew darker. Neville Chamberlain, a sick man, resigned in May to be replaced as Prime Minister by Winston Churchill.

Dee's new job was demanding. She put in as much overtime as she could, preferring to work to exhaustion rather than have too many hours to brood.

'Working long hours is praiseworthy, of course,' Mr Royce said, placing a mug of tea in front of her in the canteen. 'But if you're too exhausted you're useless to the patients.'

Dee opened her eyes and regarded him with a sleepy smile. She respected him greatly but her awe had been softened by liking. He was in his late forties, with hair already greying and a pleasant, gentle manner.

'I know,' she said, taking the mug thankfully. 'I'm leaving in a minute.'

'Do you manage to see much of your fiancé?'

'Not for a couple of weeks, although I hope he'll manage to visit us soon. The airfield isn't so far away, but of course he's mostly on call. I know I'm one of the lucky ones, because I do get to see him sometimes. The ones I feel sorry for are the women whose men are in the army, stationed in France, because they say Hitler is advancing.'

'As a matter of fact,' Mr Royce said casually, 'I can give you some news of Mark. They say he's making a name for himself, a brave and skilful pilot. You should be proud of him.'

'Thank you for telling me,' Dee said.

She didn't ask how he knew. It was common knowledge in the hospital that he had friends in high places. One rumour even said he had a cousin in the government, although nobody knew for sure. It briefly occurred to Dee to wonder how his knowledge extended as far as this one airfield, but she was too tired to think much of it.

'Mark's very pleased with himself at the moment,' she said, 'because when Winston Churchill became Prime Minister he was able to say, "I told you so".'

'He actually predicted it?'

'Not exactly, but he used to say that Churchill was the only one who knew what he was talking about.'

'That's true. Now, go home and get some sleep.'

At home she found Helen fuming, as she'd done for several weeks. There was a problem with food stocks, as ships bringing food to Britain were sunk by enemy submarines. To make supplies stretch, further ration books had been issued, directing how much could be eaten in a week.

'Four ounces of bacon,' Helen declared in disgust, 'two ounces of cheese, three pints of milk. And I have to hand over the ration book and they tear out coupons showing I've had this week's allowance and I can't have any more until I hand over next week's coupons.'

'It's to make sure everyone gets a fair share, Mum,' Dee

explained. 'Otherwise, the folk with money would buy up the lot.'

'That's all very well, but Mark's coming next weekend. How can we feed him properly?'

'I think he'll understand the problem.'

She was counting the minutes until she would see Mark, but the day before he was due to arrive the telephone rang.

'I can't come tomorrow,' he said. 'All leave has been cancelled.'

'But why?'

'I don't know, and I couldn't tell you if I did. But something big's happening, take my word.'

That was the first she heard of Dunkirk.

CHAPTER EIGHT

DUNKIRK: May 1940, a name and a date that were to become inscribed in history, but in fact few details came out at the time. It was only in hindsight that it was possible to see the story as a whole, how British and French soldiers had been driven back through France until they reached the harbour of Dunkirk, where, over nine days, more than three hundred thousand of them were rescued by a fleet of ships that had crossed the channel from England. Some were Royal Navy destroyers, but many were small vessels, merchant ships, fishing boats, lifeboats, and these were the ones that passed into legend.

Enemy planes bombarded the evacuation, and were fought off by the Royal Air Force.

'They saved thousands of lives,' Mr Royce told her, 'but their own losses were terrible, over four hundred planes. Do you have any news of Mark?'

'Yes, he called me several times to say he was all right. I'm glad I knew that before I heard about those losses. Thank goodness it's over now.'

'Dee, it's not over, it hasn't begun. Who do you think will be attacked next?'

'Us,' she said slowly. 'In this country.'

A few days later she, like many others, sat by the radio, listening to Churchill confirming their worst fears: 'The battle of France is over. I expect that the Battle of Britain is about to begin… The whole fury and might of the enemy must very soon be turned on us.'

And the front line of defence would be the Air Force.

By day she threw herself into her work, seeing Mark in every patient, finding her only solace in devoting herself to their care. At night she lay in the darkness, whispering, 'Come back to me,' and holding the little bear he'd won for her at the fair.

Now their contact was almost nil. When he could manage to telephone, the call would come when she was at work. She would arrive home to hear Helen say, 'He called. Says everything's fine and he sends his love.'

'Sends his love.' It was a neutral phrase that anyone might have used, but she treasured it nonetheless.

Mr Royce had been right in his prediction. Three weeks after Dunkirk, the Channel Islands were invaded. Two weeks later, the enemy bombers arrived over England and the Air Force was in action against them, fighting them back so ferociously that Churchill paid a public tribute that went down in history.

'Never in the field of human conflict,' he said to a packed House of Commons, 'was so much owed by so many to so few.'

The pilots were the heroes of the hour. Pictures appeared in the press showing young men, leaning casually against their planes, laughing as though danger was just something they took in their stride.

Mostly the pictures were groups, but occasionally one pilot was shown alone. That was how Dee first saw the photograph of Mark, perched on the wing of his Spitfire, relaxed and clearly exhilarated by the life he led.

'You'd think they hadn't a care in the world,' Matron observed as they studied the papers during a hurried tea break.

'Why are they all holding up their hands like that?' Dee wondered, looking at a group picture.

'That's to tell you how many enemy aircraft they've just shot down. Look at him.' She pointed to Mark, who had four fingers on display. 'You can see he's proud of himself.'

Then she gave a laugh. 'I wonder if there are any plain middle-aged pilots. If you believe the press, they're all young, handsome and dashing.'

'Some of them are,' Dee murmured.

Part of her was bursting with pride, although it was undermined by terror for his life. But she knew that this simply made her one of many, and so she was shy of speaking about it.

Even with Mr Royce she was reticent, although he'd now become a trusted confidant. If she'd had thoughts to spare for him, she might have wondered at how often they chanced to meet in the canteen, but she had no thoughts for anyone but Mark.

'How long is it since you saw him?' Mr. Royce asked one day.

'Weeks, but of course he can't get leave now.'

'But didn't you say he was at—?' He named the airfield. 'Surely there's a café nearby where you could wait for him to get a few minutes off. Let him know you're there, and that you'll wait all day if necessary.'

'But I have to be here—' she gasped.

'Leave that to me. You haven't had a day off for too long.'

By good luck, Mark chanced to call that night and she outlined the plan to him.

'That's wonderful!' he said. 'There's a little café called The Warren just outside the airfield. Wait for me there.'

Mr Royce was true to his word and for one day she was free to hurry to the airfield and settle down in the café as soon as it was open. She bought sparingly, knowing that it might be a long wait.

After a while the place began to fill up and the woman behind the counter regarded her with suspicion, even hostility. At last she approached her, glaring.

'I've got a business to run. I can't afford to have people taking up the chairs and not buying anything. You all seem to think you can use this place as a collection point.'

'All?'

'You know what I mean, and don't pretend that you don't.'

Dee did know and was half amused, half angry. 'Actually, I'm a nurse,' she said, 'and I'm waiting for my fiancé.'

The woman regarded her for a moment. 'If you're a nurse, come and take a look at my son. He's ten and very naughty. He cut himself this morning and he won't let anyone look at it.'

After that, things went well. The cut turned out to be minor and easily dressed. Her hostess visibly warmed.

'My name's Mrs Gorton. You stay here as long as you like, and I'll bring you something.'

She served Dee a lunchtime snack, on the house, and began to chat with her as the café cleared.

'Sorry about that, but you should see some of them that come in here. I suppose it can't be helped. Get a lot of young men together and the "good time girls" are going to…well… offer them a good time, if you know what I mean.'

'Yes, I know what you mean,' Dee said.

'And they do a lot of business, so I'm told. The newspapers don't tell that kind of story. Oh, no, those lads are heroes so they're all virtuous, but the two don't go together, take my word. I could tell you things well, anyway, the girls who flaunt themselves aren't the ones you have to worry about. It's the ones that look respectable, like those two near the door. What time will your fiancé be here?'

'I don't know. When he can get away. Perhaps never. No—wait—I think that's him.'

She could just see a figure in a leather jacket coming along the street. The next moment she'd leapt to her feet and hurried out to meet him. Laughing joyfully, Mark enfolded her in a bear hug and for a few minutes she forgot everything else.

'We'll have to go back inside,' he said at last. 'I can't move far.'

'I don't care where it is,' she said fervently.

As they entered she saw Mrs Gorton rise and move back to the counter. For a moment her eyes were fixed curiously on Mark and Dee realised she was conveying a warning about the two girls by the window who 'looked respectable' but clearly weren't.

It was plain what she meant. The girls were regarding Mark, wide-eyed, and in all fairness Dee couldn't blame them. In a short time he'd grown older, heavier, more adult, and a hundred times more attractive. Until now, the boy had lingered in his face, but the experience of confronting death time and again had changed him.

One of the girls seemed about to hail him, then her eyes flickered to Dee and she shrugged and turned away.

Forget it, Dee wanted to say. *He's mine.*

A young man at a corner table rose and headed for the door, passing close by. Dee frowned.

'Pete?' she queried cautiously.

He stared, then grinned when he'd recovered. 'Fancy seeing you here!' he exclaimed.

'You two know each other?' Mark asked.

'We were at school together,' Dee explained, 'although Pete was two forms above me. He saved me from bullies once.'

'Then let me shake your hand,' Mark said, doing so and giving Pete a good-natured grin.

'What are you doing here?' Dee asked him. 'Are you an airman?'

'No, I'm a mechanic,' Pete said. 'I wanted to fly, but I was useless at it. Not like him.' He indicated Mark. 'Regular mad devil, that's what they say.'

Mark grinned again, not at all troubled by this assessment.

'I'll…er…leave you alone, then,' Pete said, suddenly becoming self-conscious.

'Yes, do, there's a good chap,' Mark agreed, shepherding Dee to a table.

He sat down facing her, his hands holding hers across the table, smiling as he did in her dreams.

'I can't stay long, so let's make the most of it,' he said. 'I've missed you.'

'Has it been very bad?'

He shrugged. 'They haven't caught me yet and they're not going to.'

'But there's more to come, isn't there?'

'I'm afraid so. I worry about you, too. Are you sleeping in that Anderson shelter?'

She made a face. 'We tried it but it's so uncomfortable. Mum simply refuses to leave the house now, and we can hardly leave her there alone. To hell with Hitler!'

He touched her cheek. 'That's the spirit.'

Silence fell for a few moments and she had the strange impression that he was uneasy, which was rare with him. Then, as if coming to a sudden resolution, he said, 'I've got something for you.'

He reached into his pocket and pulled out a small box which he opened to reveal a ring.

'It's about time I gave you an engagement ring. I hope it fits.'

It fitted perfectly. It was tiny and cheap, with a small piece of glass where a diamond should have been. She wouldn't have changed it for the world.

'Hey, don't cry,' he chided, brushing her cheek. 'What happened to my sensible Dee?'

'She doesn't really exist,' she choked. 'She's just a pretence.'

'I hope not. I'll rely on her to keep me straight when this is over.'

'When it's over,' she said longingly. 'One day—but when?' To her surprise, he sighed and for a moment a bleak look came over his face. It was gone in an instant, but she knew she wasn't mistaken.

'What is it?' she asked. 'I thought you were loving it.'

'Well, some of it.'

'Being one of "the few", having your picture in the paper. After that photo appeared in the national press, the local paper used it as well. Now there's a copy hanging up in the church hall with "Our Hero" written underneath.'

'Please, Dee, you're making me blush.'

'Nonsense, I know how conceited you really are.'

'Oh, you do!'

'Yes, I do,' she said, laughing as she spoke. 'And you bask in the spotlight. Oh, Mark, what is it?' The bleak look had appeared again. 'Am I being clumsy? I'm sorry.'

'No, it's just that…well…it's not like the romantic picture they give you. When you take off, you never know what's going to happen.'

'Of course not, how stupid of me. It must be scary. Are you—?'

'Am I scared? Yes, but not in the way you think. If you get shot down it'll all be over soon. I can cope with that. It's when I shoot one of them down that it gets hard.'

His fingers tightened on her hand and she clasped him back, waiting silently.

'It's all right when they're at a distance,' he went on. 'But sometimes it happens close up and you can see them, even hear them scream over the engines as they go down to their deaths.'

'But otherwise it would be you,' she urged.

'I know. You tell yourself it's them or you but that doesn't always help. If you see their faces they've become real, and you know you've killed a man.'

'A man who was trying to kill you,' she said firmly.

'Yes. It's just a bit of a shock at first. Ah, well, never mind.'

The last words were like a barrier set up suddenly, as though he'd seen where the conversation was leading and didn't want to go there.

'Mark, please talk to me if you want to—'

'I talk too much,' he said heartily. 'I can remember when you used to say so.'

'That was in another world. If you—'

'Hey, who's that?'

There was a movement from outside the window and another airman looked in, jerking his head when he saw Mark. 'We have to get back now,' he said tensely. 'Take off in an hour.'

'Goodbye,' Mark said, rising and leaning forward to kiss her.

She had a thousand things to say. *I love you. Take care. Call me when you get back.* But she said none of them, just followed him to the door and stood watching as he walked away. The girls of easy virtue were still there and one of them tried to stop and talk to him, but he shook her off and hurried on.

Mrs Gorton came to stand beside her at the door. 'Is he your fiancé?' she asked.

'That's him,' Dee replied, her eyes on Mark's retreating figure.

She wasn't really listening to Mrs Gorton, and so missed the slight curious note in her voice. Nor did she hear the way she said, 'Hmm!' or see the pitying look the older woman gave her.

In fact she saw and heard nothing in the outside world. Now her whole universe was taken up by the feel of the ring on her finger, and joy that he'd remembered it in the middle of so much else.

There was another happiness, too. She treasured the moment when he'd come so close to confiding in her about the horrors of his job. That was what she could give him, what would draw them closer. All she needed was time. But time might yet be denied them. As night descended and she pictured him high up, making life and death decisions, she knew a return of terror and fiercely clasped the ring on her left hand.

He had said they wouldn't catch him and it seemed as if he was right. He survived that night's sortie and many others to come. Now the bombers focused all their attention on London in what became known as the Blitz. Dee and her parents took refuge in the Anderson shelter in the garden while the noise thundered around them and far off they could hear the screams of the injured and the crash of collapsing buildings. By a miracle, the Parsons' house was left standing, but when they emerged in the morning there was always devastation to be witnessed.

During that time she saw Mark once more, meeting him at the café. When he left she strolled with him as close to the airfield as possible and blew him a kiss as he vanished. The way back lay past the café. To her surprise, Mrs Gorton was waiting for her at the door.

'You've been good to me, so I thought I'd warn you,' she said. 'Are you really planning to marry that one?'

'Yes, of course.'

'Well, don't, that's all I've got to say. I told you last time how some of them carry on, but I didn't tell you he's one of the worst.'

'Nonsense!'

'Is it? Look at him. A feller like that can have any girl he wants, and don't kid yourself that he's all faithful and perfect because he isn't. He takes what's offered, like they all do.'

'Why are you trying to turn me against him?' Dee asked desperately.

'Because I like you and you deserve better. Look, my dear, I can understand that you want to grab him while you can. After all, he's a catch and you're no great beauty. No offence meant.'

'None taken,' Dee assured her quietly.

'But give him a miss. He'll break your heart.'

She could stand it no more, but fled blindly, at first not even noticing that she was heading back to the airfield. She stopped a few yards from the wire perimeter, breathing hard. In the distance she could see lights, young men coming and going, laughing. They were ready for anything but expected no call tonight. Some of the figures in shirts and trousers were actually female, taken into the Air Force to serve as mechanics. She remembered how she and Mark had shared a joke about that long ago.

And then she saw him, walking across the grass in the company of two other young men, their laughter carried on the evening air. Three young women, also in uniform, were with them, in a high state of excitement.

Suddenly Mark stopped, turned to one, took her face in his hands and delivered a smacking kiss. Then the next. Then the third, while his male companions cheered and clapped. While the girls giggled and mimed shyness.

At this distance Dee knew she couldn't be seen, but she still began to move backwards, seeking the protection of the shadows, talking sensibly to herself.

What she had seen meant nothing. Nothing at all. He hadn't kissed those girls romantically or passionately, but swiftly, one after another, in front of an audience, as if in fulfilment of a

bet. Yes, that was it. A bet. Now they were all headed for the
tent where the six of them would spend the evening together
in innocent camaraderie.

But Mark was the last one to go into the tent, held back by
a girl who grasped his hand and seemed to be pleading with
him. He was arguing, laughing, refusing her something she
wanted. Dee held her breath, knowing that the decision he
took now was crucial.

But he made no decision. The others came out, seized him
and hustled him in. The tent flap descended. Silence. Now
she would never know what he would have done.

Be sensible. You've always known he was a flirt, and these
are special conditions. Anything that happens now doesn't
count. He didn't go with her, and he probably wouldn't have
done.

But now Sylvia was there in her head, saying, *'If he wanted
to flirt, he flirted. If I showed that I minded, I was "making
a fuss about nothing".'*

Mrs Gorton seemed to be there as well, joining in the
chorus of warning, but Dee refused to listen. She began to
run in the direction of the bus stop, but when she reached it
she raced on, faster and faster, as though in this way she could
outrun the truth. She ran until she could run no more, then
slowed to a walk and groped her way through the darkness
for an hour, until she reached home.

It took a while to talk herself into calm, but she managed it.
Mark was risking his life for his country, and if he was occasionally tempted to look away from his fiancée—a fiancée
who he didn't love, she reminded herself—who knew the
strain he was under? What right did she have to judge him?

Bit by bit, she persuaded herself that she was in the wrong.
It took much effort for her sensible side kept fighting back,
saying that he was selfish and immature. After a while she
managed to silence common sense and send it slinking off

into banishment, but it cast a grim look at her, warning that it would be back.

It tried one assault in a conversation she had with Patsy, who lived in the next street, whose husband was known as a 'bit of a lad', unable to resist temptation, but always returning home in the end with a sheepish look and the plea of, 'You know it's you I really love.'

Recently she'd heard that he'd been captured and sent to a prisoner of war camp. After sighing about how much she missed him, Patsy added wryly, 'But at least now I know where he is every night.'

Dee smiled and escaped as soon as she could, but she couldn't escape the voice that said she'd just seen her own future.

There were small incidents that might mean nothing, like the weekend he was supposed to come and stay the night with the family, but cancelled at the last moment.

Be reasonable, she told herself. He's a fighter doing his duty. He can't put you first. The phrase *even if he wanted to* floated through her mind and was finally dismissed.

It was Pete who delivered the final blow. Granted a few days leave from the airfield, he sought to earn a little extra money at the garage. Joe was glad to see him. Since Mark's departure he'd been working alone and needed help.

'He's a good mechanic,' he told Dee when she came home that night. 'And I've said he must have supper with us tonight, because I knew you'd want to talk to him about Mark.'

Delighted, she hurried out to find Pete just tidying in the garage.

'Did he give you a letter for me?' she asked, 'or a message?'

He seemed embarrassed. 'No, I don't see much of him. We'd better hurry in. I promised your dad not to keep supper waiting.'

'But you can talk to me about Mark first, can't you?'

'There's nothing to say,' he said desperately. 'He's the highest of the high and I'm the lowest of the low. We don't talk.'

She waited for the desperate feeling to settle inside her, enough for her to speak calmly.

'What is it you don't want to tell me, Pete?'

'Look, it's nothing. Something and nothing.'

'Go on.'

'They all fool around—not much else to do—and Maisie's just there for the taking—it didn't mean anything, only he was a bit late getting back and the top brass got mad at him.'

'Was this two weekends ago?' she asked, referring to the time he'd been expected but didn't come.

'Yes.'

She smiled. 'Thanks, Pete. Don't worry about it, and don't mention it to my parents.'

'Look, honestly—'

'I said it's all right. The subject's closed. Finished.'

He wasn't an imaginative man, but the sight of her face alarmed him. A woman who'd aged five years in five seconds might have looked like that.

He shivered.

CHAPTER NINE

IT WASN'T easy to set up the meeting but Dee managed it, choosing another café near the airfield, not the one where they had met before and where Mrs Gorton's presence would be all too evident.

While she waited, she took a few long breaths to calm herself. What she had to do now must be done carefully, with just the perfect air of amused calm. At the last moment she felt she'd got it just right, and when Mark appeared she was able to regard him with her head on one side and a faint smile touching her lips.

'I'm glad you could find the time for me,' she teased.

'Yes, well, my commanding officer—'

'Actually, I meant Maisie.'

Only now did she understand how much she'd longed for him to deny it, but his appalled face made any such fantasy impossible.

'How the hell did you hear about that?' he demanded violently.

'Oh, you're famous for your exploits, in and out of battle.'

'Look, it meant nothing. Don't get it out of proportion. It started with just a few drinks and—'

'And Maisie came, too,' she supplied. 'These things happen, I know. It's not important.'

He regarded her curiously. 'Not important?' he echoed, as if unable to believe his ears. 'You really mean that?'

She made a wry face. 'It's not important because it brings us to a point we've been approaching for some time.'

'What do you mean?'

'Well, let's face it, this never was a real engagement, was it? You only proposed in order to shut my mother up, and I suppose I said yes for the same reason. What else could we do, caught like that? Since then we've seen so little of each other that it's just drifted, but maybe the time has come to be realistic.'

'Meaning what?' he asked in a strange voice.

'You never really wanted to marry me any more than I... well...'

'Any more than you wanted to marry me,' he supplied.

'It was an act of desperation,' she said merrily. 'You proposed marriage to get yourself out of a hole, I've always known that.'

He was very pale. 'Meaning that you think I wouldn't have gone through with it?'

'Gone through with it,' she echoed. 'That says it all, doesn't it? You only have to go through with something if it's an effort, and I think you would have done. You'd have made the effort and done your best to be a good husband. But you wouldn't have been a good husband because your heart wouldn't be in it, and I don't want a man who has to force himself.'

She paused. He was staring at her. Slowly, she lifted her left hand and slid the ring off her finger.

'I've always known you didn't love me,' she said. 'Not enough to marry. It's better to end it now.'

She held out the ring but he seemed too dazed to move.

'You're dumping me?' he asked in disbelief.

'That's all you really care about, isn't it?' she asked with a touch of anger. 'You're afraid people will know that I broke it off. Don't worry, everything's different now. You're a hero, one of "the few" and girls are queuing up for the honour of your attention. When they know you're free, they'll throw a party. You won't remember that I exist.'

She said it lightly but he stared at her in shock. 'That's the first time I've known you to say anything cruel.'

'I'm not being cruel, Mark, I'm being realistic. You'll find another girl, like you did last time. Our marriage would have been a disaster. Here.' She held the ring closer to him. 'Take it.'

Glaring, he did so. 'If that's what you want.'

'What I want,' she murmured. 'I could never tell you what I wanted. We didn't have the chance.'

'And now we never will,' he said, looking at the ring in his palm.

'Mark, when you think about it, you'll see I've done the right thing for you. You're free, as you need to be.'

'Free,' he murmured. 'Free.'

She gave him a peck on the cheek. 'Goodbye, my dear. Take care of yourself.'

As she slipped out of the door his eyes were still fixed on the ring in his hand. She couldn't even be sure that he knew she'd gone.

That night her dreams were haunted by a little boy running through an empty house, opening door after door, calling, 'Where are you?' with mounting despair.

She awoke, shivering. After that she couldn't get back to sleep, but lay weeping in the darkness.

The Blitz lasted for eight months, officially ending in May 1941, although attacks on London continued sporadically for long after.

Somehow Dee kept going. With Mark's departure, all hope seemed to have fled from her life, but there was too much work for her to brood. The hospital was overflowing with the wounded.

Even so, there were moments when she couldn't escape her thoughts, when she would lie awake longing, with every fibre of her being, for the man she'd lost. It was useless to tell herself that he'd never really loved her, that they would have had no chance and she was better off without him. Somewhere in the depths of her misery a voice whispered that she'd been too hasty, that she could have managed things better, bound him to her and won his love.

Instead, she'd done the common sense thing because that was her way. She was wise, realistic and sensible. And her heart was breaking.

She knew that a really sensible woman would discard Mad Bruin rather than keep a constant reminder of an unrequited love, but she couldn't bring herself to go quite that far.

She knew when the planes took off for a sortie because their route lay over the city. Londoners would come out and stand looking up at the sky, not always able to see the aircraft through the clouds or the darkness, but listening until the sound faded. Hours later, they would come out again to hear the return, wondering how many planes and men had been lost.

She had no news of Mark. He never wrote. He'd accepted her rejection as final.

'How's that fiancé of yours?' Mr Royce asked one day.

'I don't know. He's not my fiancé any more.'

She described their breakup briefly and without visible emotion. He listened sympathetically and never mentioned it again, except that he always seemed well informed about the activities of that particular squadron and was able to assure her that Mark was still alive and unhurt. Otherwise, she wouldn't have known.

At work her life was filled with satisfaction, yet there was no joy. In the evenings she would travel home on a bus that crawled along at a snail's pace because the whole country was under 'the blackout'. When she got off, she felt her way carefully home in the near darkness. Curtains and blinds kept the house almost invisible from the outside. Once inside, there was the relief of a small lamp.

Joe had joined the Home Guard, a civilian 'army' consisting of men who were too old to join the regular forces, or in reserved occupations such as doctors, miners, teachers and train drivers. Their job would be to fight off an invasion, and they were equipped with uniforms and weapons. Joe was proud to bursting point and regular visits to the local church hall for training sessions helped keep his spirits up.

Helen fared less well. At first Dee had been able to bring home the letters Sylvia sent to the hospital, and in this way they learned that Sylvia had given birth to a son.

'I want to go and see her,' Helen insisted.

'You can't, Mum. She's never left a return address and she didn't have the baby in hospital.'

They kept hoping but, as time passed, Helen realised that her daughter had truly rejected her and she couldn't see her grandson. Her hair rapidly became white and her eyes grew faded.

'Things will get better,' Dee tried to tell her. 'They have to. The war will end, we'll find Sylvia and the baby and we'll all be happy again.'

Helen would smile faintly but without conviction. Her health was visibly failing and she began to have dizzy spells. She always passed these off as 'nothing' and brushed aside Dee's attempts to care for her. These days, she seemed indifferent to everything and everyone.

When the blow fell, it came with shocking suddenness.

One morning, as Dee was arriving for work, the ward sister looked up urgently.

'Ah, good, there you are. Go and see the new patient in bed five. She came in two hours ago, and she keeps saying your name.'

The woman who lay there was thin and weary, with heavy

bandages on her head. All her previous beauty had fled, yet Dee knew her at once.

'Sylvia—oh, Sylvia, wake up, please.'

Sylvia opened her eyes and a faint smile touched her mouth. 'Is that really you?' she murmured.

'Yes, I'm here. I can't believe it—after all this time! Whatever happened to you?'

Her sister was in a bad way, her face bruised, her lips swollen.

'A bomb hit the house,' Sylvia murmured. 'A wall fell in on me before I could escape. They got me out in the end but—' Her voice faded.

Dee drew up a chair and leaned forward, clasping Sylvia's hand. 'Where have you been? Why didn't you let us come to see you? Mum's been worried sick.'

'I didn't want to shame her. How would she explain me to the neighbours?'

'They don't matter. It's you that matters. What about Phil? Are you still with him?'

'He died at Dunkirk. It's just me and the baby now, but—I don't know where he is. When they rescued me they must have found him as well. But where is he—*where's my baby?*' Her voice rose in anguish.

'They'll have taken him to another ward,' Dee said reassuringly. 'I'll go and ask.'

She hurried out, seizing a phone to call an ambulance official, who promised to contact her in a few minutes. Then she called her mother, who gave a little shriek on hearing the news. *'I'm coming, I'm coming. Tell her.'*

Dee returned to the ward. Sylvia's eyes had closed again and it would be best to let her sleep, at least until there was some news. A quick glance at the notes told her the worst. Sylvia had been badly injured. Her chances were poor.

'No,' Dee said to herself. 'It can't happen.'

But it could and she knew it.

She had other patients who needed her care, but while she was tending them her eyes constantly turned to the end of the ward, watching for Sylvia to wake. Part of her didn't believe this was happening. And part of her knew that the worst was going to befall her despite her resolutions.

Hurry, she whispered inwardly to her mother, *while there's still time.*

The ward sister approached and Dee explained briefly. 'My mother will be here soon and—there she is, just coming in.'

'Take care of her,' the sister said kindly. 'The others can do your work for a while.'

'Where is she?' Helen asked, running towards her in tears.

'Mum, be ready for a shock. She's badly hurt.'

Sylvia opened her eyes as her mother approached and Dee had the satisfaction of seeing them reach out to each other.

But then she saw the sister beckoning. Her face was grave. 'I'm afraid it's bad news,' she said. 'The baby was dead when they found him. They couldn't tell her because she was unconscious.'

'Oh, no,' Dee whispered. 'How can I tell her?'

Approaching the bed, she found Helen talking feverishly. 'Just as soon as you can be moved, I'm taking you home, you and the baby, and you'll live with us and we won't care what the neighbours say. Everything's going to be all right.'

'Oh, yes, please, Mum...please...you're going to love Joey. I named him after Dad.'

'He'll like that,' Helen choked. 'We're all going to be so happy.'

Dee wondered if her mother really believed this. How much did she understand? Could she see that her daughter was dying, or was she spared that for the moment?

Sylvia's eyes were closed and she was talking wildly, her breath coming in shaky gasps that were getting worse. 'Mum...Mum...'

'Yes, darling, I'm here. Hold on.'

But Sylvia was no longer capable of holding on. Her breath faded, her hands fell away.

'No!' The cry broke from Helen as she gathered her lifeless daughter in her arms. 'No, you've got to stay with me. We're going home together and I'm going to look after you… Sylvia…*Sylvia!'*

She burst into violent sobs, clutching her daughter's body and shaking it, as though trying to infuse it with life, and crying her name over and over.

Dee felt for a pulse, although she knew it was useless. Her sister was dead.

Helen had recognised the truth and gently lay her child back on the bed.

'We haven't lost her,' she choked. 'Not really. We'll look after the baby, and it'll be like she's still with us.'

'Mum—'

Helen's voice and her eyes became desperate. 'We'll do that, won't we? We must find the baby and take him home. Yes, that's what we'll do…that's what…what we…' Her breath began to come in long gasps. She clutched her throat, then her heart while her eyes widened.

'Help me,' Dee cried, supporting Helen in her arms.

Helping hands appeared. An oxygen mask was fitted over Helen's face but it was too late. The heart attack was massive and she was dead in minutes.

'Go with them,' the ward sister said as the two women were taken away to the hospital mortuary. 'Oh, my dear, I'm so sorry.'

'It was bound to happen,' Dee whispered. 'When Sylvia went away she suffered badly, but she always nursed the hope they'd be reunited. Sylvia's death destroyed her.' Tears began to run down her face. 'Oh, heavens! How am I going to tell my father? His wife, his daughter, his grandson, all on the same day.'

Now the shock was getting to her and she began to shiver uncontrollably. She was still shivering when Joe arrived at the hospital and joined her in the mortuary. His face was so pale and grey that for a dreadful moment she feared she was about to lose him, too.

She told him what had happened, adding, 'Sylvia died in her arms.'

'Then they found each other again,' he said. 'Thank God! Sylvia was always her favourite.' Then he added gently, 'Just like you were always mine.'

Until then, she'd never appreciated her father's strength, but it was a new, tougher man who told her to leave the funeral arrangements to him because, 'You've been through enough.'

And it was true—she was reaching the end of her tether. She almost gave way entirely when she and Joe stood in the mortuary regarding Sylvia with her baby in her arms, ready to be buried together. Joe's arm was strong about her, but even he nearly yielded to terrible grief at the sight of the child.

'My grandson,' he whispered as tears streamed down his face. 'My first ever grandchild, and we meet like this. Poor Sylvia. Poor Helen.'

They supported each other through the three-way funeral, and afterwards Joe put his arms around her. 'We've both lost everyone else,' he said huskily. 'There's just us now, love.'

Like others who had suffered devastating losses, Dee and her father survived as day passed into day, week into week and month into month. He'd said they had just each other, and for now neither of them wanted anyone else. Christmas 1942 was their first alone, and they were thankful to pass it quietly, refusing all invitations.

These days she relied totally on Mr Royce for news of Mark, so that when she went in one morning in the new year to find him looking grave, she knew what had happened.

'I'm sorry,' he said.

'He's dead, isn't he?' she said bleakly.

For a moment the world went dark. She clutched the back of a chair, then felt him supporting her until she sat down.

'No,' he said. 'He isn't dead.'

'*Not dead?* Do you mean that?'

'I swear to you that he's alive, but he's very badly hurt. His Spitfire was hit during a battle. He just managed to limp home but, as he landed, the plane burst into flames. They brought him here. He's lucky to be alive.'

'But he is alive—and he's going to stay alive, isn't he? *Isn't he?*'

'I think so.' The words were cautious.

'But it's not certain?'

'He's been very badly burned and he needs help. It's lucky you're here. The sight of you will help him.'

'Where is he?'

'Come this way.'

As they went along the corridor he said, 'I've had him put in a separate ward. I'd better warn you that he looks pretty alarming. He was engulfed in flames. It was a miracle that his face escaped. His helmet saved him, but he has burns all over his torso, and an injury to the head where he hit it.'

She paused as they reached a door, Mr Royce pushing it open quietly and standing aside.

Dee approached slowly, and gradually the bed came into view. Then she stopped, appalled, shaking at the sight. In her worst nightmares she hadn't imagined this.

The man on the bed could have been anybody, so totally was he covered in bandages. They extended over his torso, his arms, up over his neck and around his head.

Where was the daredevil young hero who laughed in the face of danger? Gone—and in his place lay this helpless baby. She wanted to cry aloud to the heavens that it wasn't fair of life to do this to him. Why was there nobody to defend him?

But there was, she thought with sudden resolution. She was here now. She would defend him.

'Has he been unconscious all the time?' she asked softly.

'No, he's come round and muttered something, but of course most of the time we keep him heavily sedated against the pain.' Mr Royce examined a chart. 'Going by the time of his last injection, he should come round quite soon.'

'You can leave me alone with him,' Dee said. 'He'll be safe with me.'

'I'm sure he will.'

When the door had closed, Dee came closer to the bed. As a nurse, she was used to horrific sights, but nothing in her experience helped her now. This was the man she loved, lying alone and in agony.

His eyes were closed and his breathing came with a soft rasping sound that was almost like a groan. Now she could see just enough of his face to recognise him. The mouth was the one she knew, wide and made for laughter, but tense now, as though the pain reached him, even in sleep.

Dee drew a chair forward and sat down, leaning as close to him as she could get. 'Hello, darling,' she whispered.

Nothing. He didn't move or open his eyes, but lay almost like a dead man.

'It's me—Dee,' she persisted. 'I heard you'd been injured, and I had to come and see you. Even after what happened, we're still friends, aren't we? You still matter to me, and I want to see you well and strong again.'

Silence but for his soft breathing. No sign of life. Refusing to be put off, she continued, 'You really will be all right in the end, although it may take some time. They say you're pretty badly hurt, but I've nursed men with worse injuries and they come through it because they can't wait to get up there in the sky again.'

She was stretching the truth here. She knew how unlikely it was that Mark would ever return to being an airman, and how long it would be before he could live any kind of normal life, but she couldn't afford to think of that. Only one thing mattered and that was bringing him back into the land of the living. If she could do that, and even one day see him smile again, she cared for nothing else.

She went on, forcing herself to sound cheerful. 'I wish we were still engaged. Oh, don't think I'm trying to trap you. You were always too clever to be caught by any woman. But you don't seem to have anyone of your own.'

The truth of that struck her with force. The star of the squadron, the man every girl wanted to flirt with, and more. But he had nobody; no family, nobody had been allowed to get close to him. Except herself. She had crept closer than anyone, yet even she hadn't suspected his essential aloneness before now. He'd always worked so hard to conceal it.

Had he done so knowingly? she wondered. Had he really understood himself that well? Somehow she doubted it. Whatever Mark's qualities, insight wasn't one of them. That was why he had needed her. But she hadn't seen it either, and had rejected him.

'Are you glad I came to see you?' she asked him. 'I hope you are. I know you're asleep but maybe you can hear me, somewhere deep inside you, and perhaps…perhaps your heart is open to what I want to say. Oh, I do hope so because there's so much I want you to understand.

'I was clumsy before. I loved you so much that I was afraid to let you know, in case it embarrassed you. You see, I knew you didn't love me—well, maybe a little, but not as I love you. I was so happy when you asked me to marry you that I didn't let myself worry about how it happened. All I saw was that I could be your wife.

'I was fooling myself, but I wouldn't face it because you were everything to me. And when I did face it—I went a bit crazy. I blamed you for not loving me, but you can't love to order. Nobody can. You have to accept people as they are, or back off. I backed off. I thought I was doing what you wanted. Now I'm not so sure. Perhaps I still have something to give you—something that you need.'

A soft rumble came from between his lips, almost as though he was signalling agreement. Of course, that was fanciful, which she never allowed herself to be. But perhaps, just this once—

'Oh, darling, if only I could believe that you hear me and know what I'm trying to say. I came here as soon as I knew you were hurt because if there's anything I can do for you, I'll do it. It doesn't matter what it is. Do you understand that? Anything at all.'

She looked down at his hands lying on the blanket; one bandaged, the other uncovered. How fine and well shaped it was. How well she remembered it touching her, teasing softly through her thin clothes, making her want him in ways that she knew she shouldn't.

Inching her way forward cautiously, she took his free hand in hers, caressing it softly with her fingers. He neither moved nor showed any sign of a response, and her heart ached to see his power reduced to this helplessness. She would have given everything she possessed to see him restored to his old self— mischievous, disrespectful, outrageous, infuriating, magical. Even if it meant that she would lose him again, if her heart broke a thousand times over, she would accept it if, in return, she could see him happy.

'You're going to get better,' she told him, more confidently than she felt. 'You can count on that because I won't settle for anything else. I can be a bully when I set my mind to it, and that's what I'm going to do. You told me once you weren't good at taking orders, but you'll take mine. Get well! There! That's an order, do you hear?'

She struggled to keep the jokey note in her voice, but at last it was more than she could bear. Her words trembled into silence and she laid her face against his hand while the tears flowed.

'Come back to me,' she whispered. 'Come back to me. I love you with all my heart. I'll never love anyone else. You don't have to love me. Just let me care for you.'

After a while she raised her head again and looked closely at the man who lay without moving, barely breathing.

'I have to believe that somewhere, deep inside your heart, you can hear me,' she told him. 'Perhaps you're even conscious of it now, and soon you'll wake and remember. Or perhaps my words will come back to you without you even knowing how or when you heard them. Oh, my love, my love, can I creep into your heart without you even noticing, and then just stay there?'

A long sigh came from him. Summoning all her courage, she laid her lips gently against his. 'I thought I'd never kiss you again,' she murmured. 'Can you feel me? Can you feel my love reaching out to you? It's yours if you want it.'

Another sigh. She looked down on him tenderly. 'Yes, oh, yes,' she breathed. 'You're coming back to me. You are.'

Her joy soared as Mark opened his eyes. For a long moment they looked at each other.

'Who are you?' he asked.

CHAPTER TEN

FOR a long time now everything in his life had been jagged. It started with the danger that threatened whenever he took to the air, but he accepted that. It was the life he'd chosen. But then he found that the sunlight was jagged and threatening, making him reluctant to face it. Worst of all was the soft jaggedness of darkness and the insidious fear that kept him awake, all the more alarming because he didn't understand it.

It had started when she broke their engagement. He'd been cool and self-contained, as befitted a man who could have any woman, shrugging off her desertion. She'd set him free. She'd said so herself, predicting that the other women would throw a party.

'You won't remember that I exist,' she'd said.

Then the numbness that shielded him had begun to disintegrate and a spark of temper had flared. He'd accused her of cruelty, something he'd never felt from any woman before. When she'd gone the anger stayed with him, making him act unlike himself. He'd gone drinking with friends that night, casually remarking that his engagement was over. One of the others, a hearty, shallow young man called Shand, had made the mistake of congratulating him. Overwhelmed by rage, Mark had launched himself on the imbecile and might have killed him if his friends hadn't hauled him off in time.

After that, everyone regarded him differently. His friends kept watchful, protective eyes on him, lest he break out again. From Shand he received awe and respect, which disgusted him.

'Well, at least someone managed to shut the little blighter up,' Harry Franks observed once. Harry had joined the Air Force on the same day as Mark and they had immediately become friends. 'You should be proud of that.'

'He's not worth it,' Mark snapped.

'I agree. But he might have hit the nail on the head. Maybe you really are better off without this girl. You aren't in love with her, are you?'

'How the hell do I know?' Mark roared.

Harry nodded wisely, his expression suggesting that if he'd known things were like that, he wouldn't have asked.

Mark's inner fury continued, all the worse because he didn't understand it himself. Dee had broken the engagement in a way that suggested that he was really dumping her, thus preserving his dignity. So what was there to be angry about? Especially with her?

But he knew that if she were here this minute, he would explain to her exactly why she was wrong about everything, make her admit it and ask his forgiveness for misjudging him. Then he would replace the ring on her finger as a symbol of his victory. It was the only way to deal with awkward women.

'We belong together,' he rehearsed. 'We've always known what each other was thinking, and that's never happened to me with anyone else. I didn't want it before. I've tried to keep my thoughts to myself because I didn't trust anyone else, but with you I couldn't do that and I didn't mind. I even liked it. Do you realise that? You did something for me that…that… and then you abandoned me.'

No, he couldn't say these things. They sounded pathetic, and at all costs he wasn't going to be pathetic. But there were other ways of putting it so that she would see reason. If only she was here!

But she wasn't, and she didn't contact him.

He even began to jot down his thoughts, to be ready to confront her. But it was a fraught business. He slept at the base, sharing a small dormitory with five others, all ready for action at any moment in the night. It was hard to find privacy and if he heard someone coming he had to stuff his papers into a small cupboard by the bed. Once he did this so hastily that the contents of the overfull cupboard fell out and he found himself confronting a small bear in a frilly dress.

It was the one she'd given him at the fun fair, having bought it for the ludicrously expensive price of one shilling and sixpence.

Dee seemed to be there, teasing him out of the jagged darkness. 'She's going to keep an eye on you…and report back to me if you get up to mischief.' Then her voice changed, became loving, as he remembered it. 'And look after you.'

'Are you reporting back to her now?' he murmured. 'I wonder what you'll tell her.'

Then he stopped short, wondering at himself, knowing how it would have looked if any of his comrades had caught him talking to a toy.

But not her. She would have understood. Did she still talk to the Mad Bruin he'd given her? Did she still have it? He found himself hoping that she did. But of course he would never know.

The sound of the door opening made him quickly hide the bear. This was private, between Dee and himself, the one thing that still united them across the miles and the silence. In an obscure way, it was a comfort to a man who'd never admitted to himself that he needed to be comforted.

He hadn't given the toy a name, but in his mind she became 'Dee'. Incredibly, there was even a physical resemblance. Not that the little bear had Dee's features, but she had her expression—wry, teasing, unconvinced, a look that could be summed up as, *Oh, yeah?* Which was absurd if you thought about it, but he didn't think about it. He just appreciated it.

He began to keep his little friend with him, unwilling to leave her in the locker where she might be discovered. An inner pocket in his loose flying jacket made a useful hiding place and one day, almost forgetting she was there, he took her onto the plane with him.

It was a fierce and terrible sortie, a bombing raid on an enemy armaments factory in early 1943. Resistance was fierce, with Messerschmitts, the magnificent enemy bombers, attacking from all directions. At one point he would almost have sworn he'd reached his final moment, when the plane heading for him seemed to halt in mid-air before exploding in a ball of fire. He had a searingly precise view of the pilot's desperate eyes before the other plane dropped out of the sky.

When he landed he sat for a moment, arms folded across his body, feeling the little bump beneath the flying jacket that told him his tiny friend was there. To think that 'Dee' had protected him was sheer fanciful madness, and he wasn't a fanciful man, yet the thought persisted. *She* had been there, not the woman herself, but her little furry representative. It was crazy. He was a fool, a stupid, naive, delusional idiot. Yet he was also mysteriously comforted.

After that, the bear went with him on every sortie, seeing him through near-misses, escapes and the odd triumph. And it began to seem to Mark that Dee—his own true Dee, the woman who had scorned him—had nevertheless the right to know that she was influencing his life, perhaps even saving it. It was an excuse to write to her, and he badly needed an excuse.

The letter was hard. On light matters he'd always found talking easy—too easy—but now, in the depths of sincerity, he found the words eluding him. He wrote at last:

I meant to send her back to you, but she's a nice little companion and I'd miss her. Do you still have the Mad Bruin? Do you ever look at him and think of me? I hope so. You were right to break it off. I'm a useless character and I'd be no good for you, but let him remind you of me sometimes; even if it's only the annoying things, like how unreliable I am, no common sense, the way I make jokes about all the wrong things, don't turn up when I'm expected, stick my nose in where it's not wanted, never seem to understand when you want to be left alone. I'm sure you can think of plenty more.

The letter didn't satisfy him. It didn't even begin to convey what was in his heart, but he wasn't even sure what that was. And, even if he had been sure, he didn't think he could have said it. He put the paper away, to be finished later.

He did return to it several times, always remembering something else that it was vital for her to know. Days passed, then weeks, and somehow it was never sent.

He was afraid and he knew it. The man who faced down death a hundred times was afraid to contact the woman whose reply could damage him more than any Messerschmitt. Afraid! How she would laugh at that. And, after all, she had the right to know that she'd triumphed, just as she had the right to know that she was protecting him. Perhaps he could simply turn up and confront her with it, and watch her face as she learned exactly what she'd done to him. The temptation was so strong that he shut his thoughts off abruptly.

Another sortie was beginning, demanding his attention. He took off in the sunlight, headed out over the sea towards the continent. After that, things became confused. He knew his aircraft was hit and he was aware of himself mechanically piloting back to England and safety, frantically praying that he would arrive before the explosion.

He almost made it. As he came down the flames were beginning to take over. Another few seconds...just a few... just a few...

Then the air was rent by a terrible screaming that he didn't even recognise as his own. The jaggedness converged on him from all directions, stabbing, burning, terrifying him. Hands were tearing at the plane, pulling him out. He lay on the ground, listening to the shouting around him, waiting for his life to end. It was all over now and the only thing that really hurt was that he would never see Dee again. Then the darkness engulfed him.

But, instead of swallowing him up for ever, it lifted after a while, revealing a mist, with her voice all around him. He couldn't see her face but her words filled his heart with joy.

'…Maybe you can hear me, somewhere deep inside you… there's so much I want you to understand…'

He tried to speak but he could make no sound. Her voice continued whirling through the clouds.

'I was clumsy before. I loved you so much that I was afraid to let you know… I was so happy when you asked me to marry you… All I saw was that I could be your wife…'

My wife, he thought. You are my wife, now and always. Why can't I tell you?

'Come back to me… I love you with all my heart… Just let me care for you.'

Everything in him wanted to say yes, to find her, draw her close. He opened his eyes in desperate hope, straining to see her face, which must be full of the same emotion as her voice, an emotion that offered him hope for the first time in his life.

But his dream had been in vain. There was only a nurse in a professional uniform, the cap low over her forehead, her features frowning and severe. Disappointment tore him, making him say almost violently, *'Who are you?'*

At first the words made no impact on Dee. She couldn't understand them—*wouldn't* understand them and their terrible implication.

He stared at her, or perhaps through her. His eyes were empty of recognition, of feeling, of anything.

'Who are you?'

'I...Mark, it's me...Dee...'

But his eyes remained blank until he closed them, murmuring, 'Sorry, Nurse.'

She took a deep breath, telling herself that it meant nothing. She was in uniform, her hair covered by a nurse's cap, as he hadn't seen her before. And he was heavily sedated, not his normal self.

'Nurse—' he murmured.

'Yes, I'm here.'

He gave a long tortured sigh that ended in a groan.

Mr Royce came quietly into the room. 'He's due for more painkiller,' he said. 'Will you help me administer it?'

Together they did what was necessary, which seemed to bring Mark some ease. He opened his eyes again, murmuring, 'Thank you, Nurse.'

'Leave him to sleep,' Mr Royce said, ushering her out of the room.

'He doesn't know me,' she said flatly when they were outside.

'Given the condition he's in, that's hardly surprising, but part of his recovery will be regaining the memories of his old life and you can assist him in that as nobody else can. I'm assigning you to him full-time. Yes, I know that will be hard for you, but you must be professional about this, Nurse.'

'Of course.'

Professional, she told herself. That was what mattered. She must forget her shame at the memory of the things she'd said, the impassioned outpouring of love, the naive way she'd hoped for some flicker of love in return, only to be met with 'Who are you?'

She took immediate charge of him, silencing all other thoughts but his need and her duty, but it was hard when he feelings were so involved. The first time she saw his burns she had to fight back tears. The whole of his chest was violently red and raw, and she could only guess at what he must be suffering. Her ministrations made him wince, despite being on such a heavy dose of painkiller that he never seemed more than vaguely awake. Now and then he would gaze at her as though trying to remember where he'd seen her before, but he always addressed her as 'Nurse'.

'Perhaps you should stay with him overnight,' Joe told her late one evening. He'd been on a training session and they had arrived home at nearly the same moment.

'What about you?' she said, looking around at the bleak, echoing house. 'I don't like leaving you alone.'

'I'm a big boy now, love. I can cope. And I'm not alone, not really. Your Mum's here with me. No, don't look like that. I'm not mad. This is the home she created, and every inch of it is what she made. If I work late in the garage, she puts her head around the door and says, "Are you coming in or are you going to be here all night?" If I'm making tea, I always fill the pot in case she wants one. I know how much she loved me, and she still does, almost as much as I love her.'

'I always wondered about that—' Dee said hesitantly. 'The way your marriage came about—'

'Oh, you mean that stuff about me making her pregnant and being forced to do the decent thing. Nah, nobody forced me. I was daft about her, but I was shy. I was even scared to kiss her in case she was offended, while as for…you know…'

'Yes, I know,' she said, lips twitching.

'All right, go on, laugh at me, but it was another age. You were supposed to behave yourself in them days. But your mum knew what she wanted, and she wanted me. Lord knows why, but she did.'

'Are you saying—?'

'She made the running. I wouldn't have dared.'

Dee stared, barely able to believe what she was hearing.

'So when you and she…she was the one who…? But I don't understand. She was always so strait-laced, saying we must be "good girls" and the way she acted when Sylvia went away with Phil—'

'People often do that,' Joe observed. 'Talk one way, act another. It was Sylvia's disappearing that she really minded, and the fact that she went off with a married man. She'd have forgiven her the other thing, because it was what she did herself. She told me later that she was determined to start a baby so that I'd have to stop dithering like a twerp and make my mind up,' Joe said with pride. 'She really loved me, you see.'

'Yes, she did,' Dee agreed.

'And when you've found the right one, do what you have to. So you get on with it, girl. And don't you worry about your mum and me. We'll be all right here together.'

Armed with Joe's encouragement, she began staying overnight at the hospital, sleeping in the Nurses' Home so that she could spend as much time with Mark as possible. She fed him, changed his dressings, soothed him when he half awoke, listened to his soft moans at night.

Gradually the amount of painkiller he needed lessened, and he began to sleep more peacefully. The bandages were removed from his head, and Dee marvelled at how little he seemed to have changed. The burns on his body were terrible, but his face was undamaged. To the outside world he would seem the same handsome young man he had always been, a little older, a little more weather-beaten, but basically the same. Yet this was an illusion. The damage might be hidden, but it was there.

She checked his pulse, wondering if he would awaken soon, and would he still ask who she was? Would she be nothing but the nurse who cared for him, without individuality, no different from any other? Would he even recognise her as that?

He stirred and she laid his hand down on the sheet, waiting until at last he opened his eyes, looking straight into hers.

'Hello,' he whispered.

'Hello.' She sat beside him, smiling and trying to seem cheerful.

'Where am I?'

She gave him the name of the hospital, wondering if he would recognise it as the one where she worked, but he said nothing. 'You've been here nearly a week,' she added.

'What happened to me?'

'You crashed. I'm afraid you're badly burned. Are you in pain now?'

'No, I just feel dizzy. I don't know anything.' He gazed at her intently. 'You've been looking after me, haven't you?'

'You remember that?'

'I know I've seen you somewhere before. You're Nurse—?'

'Nurse Parsons,' she said.

'Oh, yes—you were always there—and someone else—I'm trying to remember—did anyone come to visit me while I was unconscious?'

'Your commanding officer came, and a couple of your comrades looked in. I couldn't let them stay long. They just wanted to see for themselves that you're alive.'

'Nobody else?' he whispered, and she wondered if she only imagined that his voice was full of hope.

'Nobody else. Was there someone else you wanted to see? Can I find them for you?'

He sighed softly. 'Thanks, but no. She wouldn't want you to.'

'You don't know that,' Dee said quickly. 'If she's a good friend, who cares what happens to you—'

'A good friend,' he echoed with a wry smile. 'She was the best friend I had, but I didn't know it.'

'But if you know it now, perhaps she'd like to hear you say so.'

'I doubt it. Where she was concerned, I talked too much and said all the wrong things—did all the wrong things, too. She was glad to be rid of me.'

'You can't be sure of that.'

'I can. She despised me. She made that very clear.'

'She probably didn't mean it that way.'

'When a woman tells a man to go and jump in the lake, there's no doubt what she means.'

'She actually used those words?'

'Words that meant the same. She dressed it up, practically made it sound as though I was the one breaking it off, but that was just her way of smoothing things. The truth is, she despised me.' He gave a sigh. 'And she may have been right.'

'No, she didn't despise you.'

'You can't know that.'

Then inspiration came to her. Turning the lights out so that there was only the one small bedside lamp, she returned to sit beside him, turning so that her face was in shadow. Perhaps now she looked no more than a shadowy presence, and that might be the trigger.

'But I do know that,' she said.

He stared at her, startled. 'What do you know?'

'Everything she knows. You'll understand soon, when the drugs wear off.'

'Dee? Is that really you? I think…I'm beginning to understand now. Put the light on.'

She shook her head. 'Better not.' She didn't want him to see how shaken she was, eyes brimming in relief, that he had finally recognized her again.

'You're right,' he said after a moment. 'It's strange how I know you now that I can't see you properly.'

'You never did see me properly,' she murmured.

'What do you mean by that?'

'Nothing,' she said quickly. 'It's all in the past now. We're not really the same people that we were then. When did we last see each other? A year ago?'

'Longer,' he murmured. 'Much longer. It seems to stretch back for ever, into another life—'

'I know, it feels like that to me too, but it's just a year. So much has happened since.'

Tentatively, he stretched out his hand and she took it between hers. 'I've sometimes dreamed that it was you,' he said huskily. 'I've even tried to pretend that it was—but I told myself I was being foolish because you must still be angry with me.'

'I was never angry with you.'

'You gave me back my ring.'

'Not from anger. I just thought our paths were leading away from each other. We're still friends.'

'Are we? When I was injured, I was sure you'd come to me at once. When you didn't, I knew you hadn't forgiven me.'

'But I did come to you, as soon as I heard you were here. You were unconscious, so I sat and talked to you, praying for you to wake, but then you did wake and you didn't know me. You asked who I was. I said I was Dee but that meant nothing to you. The accident had wiped me from your memory.'

'No, nothing could do that. I've been in a dream. You were there, yet you weren't. I could hear you talking to me, saying things that—'

'Yes?'

He screwed up his eyes as though fighting an inner battle.

'I don't know,' he said desperately. 'They made me happy but when I awoke, I couldn't remember them. Was it you? Did you really say everything I heard?'

'How can I tell?' she said lightly. 'Since I don't know what you heard.'

'It was…it was…oh, dear God!' He closed his eyes desperately. 'Tell me. Say it again so that I'll know.'

'Not just now,' she said gently. 'You're going to be here for some time, and we'll take it step by step.'

'But you'll be here, too? You will, won't you?' His grip was tight enough to be painful.

'Yes, I'll be here. Hey, don't break my fingers or I'll be no use.'

He released her at once, letting his hand fall on the blanket in a way she would have called helpless if it had been any other man. Now his expression was resigned and she knew he'd accepted her words and manner as a rejection. If only she could take him into her arms and tell him of her love, which was stronger than ever. But instinct told her he wasn't strong enough to stand it right now. There would be a long road until he was ready, but they would travel that road together and discover where it led.

Now it was she who set the terms, guiding him through the days that followed as a friend and nurse, but with no hint of a lover, and had the satisfaction of seeing him relax and allow himself to be cared for. It hurt to see him so docile and unlike his old vibrant, cocky self, but it helped her take charge, which she was determined to do.

Now she was sleeping in the Nurses' Home, she could slip in to see him at night, staying with him in the semi-darkness, sometimes talking, sometimes silent. It was on one of these nights that she told him about Sylvia and Helen.

'Did that man ever marry her?' he asked.

'No, he couldn't get a divorce. In fact, I went to the street where they'd been living and spoke to some of the neighbours who'd survived the bombing, and they seemed to think he was planning to go back to his wife.'

'Poor Sylvia,' he said huskily. 'She deserved better. Did you ever see the baby?'

'Yes, he was in her arms when we buried them. She had nothing left to live for. I still find it hard to take in. When we were children she was so glorious, she was like queen of the world. She was going to have everything; we all thought so.'

Mark didn't answer directly but he looked sad, and she wondered what memories were troubling him now. But she would never ask. After a while, she bid him goodnight and crept away.

He'd been lucky in that the third-degree burns were on the front of his body where the fire had exploded. The seat had partly protected his back until he'd managed to fight his way out and collapse, which was good, Dee thought thankfully, because if his back had been in the same appalling state as his front he could never have lain down.

His chest was a mass of dark red blisters which she would anoint gently, trying not to hurt him, although she knew that there would be a certain amount of nerve damage that would save him from some of the pain. Sometimes Mr Royce would come in and stand watching before inviting her outside to discuss the case.

'He's doing well,' he told her. 'But there's only so far that his condition can improve. An Air Force doctor will be coming to see him soon.'

'They're not trying to get him back?' she asked, scandalised.

'Quite the reverse. I think they'll judge him unfit to return to the Force in any capacity.'

'Thank God!' she said fervently.

He regarded her for a moment. 'It matters that much?' he asked at last.

'I hate patching them up so that they can go and get killed,' she said defensively. 'At least he's one that will live.'

He was giving her a look she didn't understand and she escaped quickly back into Mark's room. She found him lying still, with a shadow in his eyes.

'When shall I congratulate you?' he asked.

'What do you mean? I'm not due for promotion for ages.'

'You're due for promotion to Mrs Royce, very soon.'

'Will you stop talking nonsense?'

'I know what I see. That man's in love with you.'

'Nonsense! He's a kind person who's gone out of his way to help me.'

But then she remembered Mr Royce's strange look a moment ago, the trouble he'd always taken to discover news of Mark. Did he do this for everyone? How could there be time? And if it was just for her—why?

'He must be twenty years older than me,' she protested. 'More.'

'So what? He's strong, mature, settled. He can offer you a position in the world. You were made to be a successful man's wife. He's in love with you.'

'You're making fun of me. You couldn't possibly tell.'

'I can, easily. When a man gets that look in his eyes, it means just one thing.'

'It's not like you to be fanciful.'

'It wasn't,' he sighed. 'But maybe it is now. What is "like me", Dee? You tell me, because I don't know any more. At night I lie here and listen to the things in my head, and I don't know what to make of them. Nothing is the way I thought. Everything is different, but I don't know what it all means. Can't you tell me?'

'My dear,' she said gently, 'how can I tell you when I've never been there, seen the things you've seen—?'

'Done the things I've done,' he finished for her. 'You're right. It must remain a mystery, more to me than anyone. But—' he assumed a cheerful air, as though forcing himself to rally '—I won't let you distract me from Mr Royce. Any day now, he'll propose, mark my words.'

'Will you stop talking nonsense, please?' she asked crisply. 'I want to finish your dressing.'

'But you—'

'Keep still and *keep quiet*,' she said, with a sharpness rare in her.

He did so, but continued to study her curiously. She finished the job and departed as soon as she could.

Deny it as she might, she was left with the uncomfortable feeling that Mark had seen something that had entirely escaped her. And the next time she talked with Mr Royce she felt uneasy, wondering what he was thinking. When their meeting ended she began to walk away, then looked back to say something and found him still watching her with an unguarded look.

The Air Force doctor made two visits and examined Mark thoroughly, especially his damaged hand. The verdict came by letter two days later.

'Invalided out,' Mark groaned, showing her the letter in disgust. 'Useless!'

He tried to flex his hand, whose limited movement had proved his undoing, more than the burns to his chest.

'You'd have had a hard time controlling a plane with that,' Dee said. 'They had to do this. At least they'll allow you something to live on.'

'A pension, you mean,' he said in disgust. 'That says all that needs to be said. I'm a pensioner.'

It was Joe who cheered him up slightly. He'd paid several visits, and the next day he dropped in again.

'I hate to admit it,' he said, glancing over the letter, 'but this is good news for me. I haven't been able to find a decent replacement for you in the garage. They're either useless or they leave. But now you can come back, and I'll be glad to have you. We can put you up in the house, so you won't have a journey to work.'

'But I'll be useless, too,' Mark said, holding up his damaged hand.

'You won't have to fly a plane with that, just rework the

movements so that you can do them differently. Lucky it's your left hand.'

'Joe, I can't take charity.'

'It's not charity. You'd be doing me a favour. That house is empty without Sylvia and Helen. It echoes something horrible. But if you're there, it'll be more cheerful.'

Mark was still uncertain, fearful of being pitied but eager for the chance to work. Dee slipped out, leaving them to it. When she met up with Joe later, he was triumphant.

'I told him you'd be there sometimes to keep an eye on him, so they might let him out of this place sooner. That did it. He's going potty in here.'

'You're a cunning schemer,' she told him lovingly.

'That's what your mum used to say, just like you said it. I told you once before—you have to know what you want and go for it.'

'And you think you know what I want?'

'Actually, love, I was thinking more of what *I* want. That house really is lonely, so a couple of grandchildren would suit me down to the ground, just as soon as you can get round to it.'

'Dad! You're shameless.'

'Got to be. No time to waste. There's a war on. Hadn't you heard?'

Chuckling to himself, he fled her wrath.

CHAPTER ELEVEN

MR ROYCE was understanding. 'Your father's right. It'll help him to go home and live a more normal life, and you can look after him. I don't suppose you'll be sleeping here any more?'

'No, I'll be spending my nights at home now,' she said.

He sighed and gave her a wry smile. 'Just as I thought. Well, good luck.'

For a moment it was all there in his eyes, everything he'd felt but never said over the last few years. Then the shutters came down and he was once more Mr Royce, figure of authority.

Mark came home a week later and was installed in Sylvia's old room. By now he was on his feet and able to take the bus with the assistance of Joe, who closed the garage for the afternoon to help him. They both reached home safely, followed in the evening by Dee.

Joe had even cooked the supper for her and they celebrated together, toasting each other in cups of tea. Then she ordered Mark to bed and he obeyed with comical meekness.

Over the next few weeks, things improved. Mark's burns healed slowly but steadily. He could still manage many tasks in the garage, and having something to occupy his mind did him good.

Life settled into a pattern that was so strangely comfortable it seemed predestined. There was even a kind of happiness in the situation. Often Dee would awaken in the small hours and lie reflecting comfortably that Mark was there, safe under the same roof. It wasn't the relationship she'd dreamed of, but it brought out the protective side of her nature. Whatever might happen in the future, he was here now, hers, to be looked after and kept from harm.

It was nearly five years since they had met and both of them had changed. The changes in him were clear enough, but she often wondered how she seemed to him. Surveying herself in the mirror, she saw no sign of the naive girl she'd once been. The person who looked back was a woman, settled in her successful career, in her life, and so mature that it was hard to believe she was only twenty-two.

One day, in the late afternoon, when Joe was out at a training session with the Home Guard and Mark was working in the garage, she made a cup of tea and was preparing to take it to him when a shadow appeared in the back door. It was Eileen, a young woman of her own age who lived a couple of streets away.

'I just thought I'd drop in and see how you were,' she said. 'Haven't seen you for ages.'

She was one of the crowd of girls who had sighed over Mark in the early days and, although she now devoted a respectable amount of time to chattering about nothing, Dee wasn't surprised when she brought the conversation round to him.

'I hear you've got Mark living here again. Fancy that.'

'He's working at the garage with Dad, and he boards here because it's convenient.'

'Oh, I'm longing to see him!'

'Come on, then. I'm just taking him a cup of tea.'

From outside the garage, they could hear Mark singing tunelessly. There was no sign of him as they entered, only the noise coming from under a large car. Suddenly the noise stopped and Mark slid out from underneath. Dee heard a sharp intake of breath beside her and turned to see Eileen, her eyes fixed on Mark in horror.

Because of the warm day, he'd removed his shirt and his bare chest was visible. Eileen's hands were pressed to her mouth and she was slowly shaking her head as though to say it couldn't be true. Then she turned and hurried away.

The sight of Mark's face as he understood that a young woman had fled from him in disgust, repelled by his disfigurement, made Dee want to commit murder. She slammed down the mug of tea and turned to pursue Eileen but Mark stopped her.

'Let her go,' he said wearily. 'I must have given her a shock. I'm sorry; I wasn't expecting anyone except you, and you're used to the sight. I forget how dreadful I must look to anyone else.'

'She had no right—'

'It wasn't her fault,' Mark said simply.

He pulled on his shirt, buttoning it up to the neck so that none of the scars were visible. Then he sat down and dropped his head into his hands.

'Just give me a little time to get used to it,' he groaned. 'It's not the first time. It happened one day at the hospital. You were away for a moment and a nurse looked in with some dressings. I think she was a student, and not used to confronting horrors.'

'You're not—'

'I know what I am. Don't give me false hope. I'm like this for life and the sooner I accept it the better. If you could have seen that student's face when she saw me… She went pale.'

'Why didn't you tell me about it?'

'Because there would have been no point. This is the reality. This is what I am now, a man who makes women turn from him in horror.'

Dee was still consumed by anger on his behalf, and it

drove her to do something that caution might otherwise have prevented.

'Not this woman,' she said, taking his face in her hands and laying her lips on his.

She was inexperienced. Beyond a few brief pecks, she'd known no other kisses but his and they seemed long ago. But now everything in her seemed to be alive with the awareness of his need, telling her how to move her lips against his so that he would know she cared for him, wanted him.

She tried to speak of desire so intense that his terrible scars couldn't kill it, and for a few moments she thought she'd succeeded. His hands reached for her, touched her tentatively at first, then firmly, eagerly. She could feel him trembling. But then he stiffened, putting his hands on her arms and pushing her gently away.

'No,' he said hoarsely. 'Not this.'

'I'm sorry,' she stammered, swamped by shame. 'I only—'

'You only thought you'd carry your nursing a bit further, didn't you? Pity the poor patient, don't let him suspect how disgusting he is. It's all part of the cure. Well, I don't want your pity, do you hear? I don't want anyone's pity. I don't even want my own, and that's tough because I'm drowning in self-pity and I don't know how to—' He shuddered. 'Oh, to hell with you! Why did you have to do that?'

Thrusting her aside, he stormed to the door, stopped and looked back. 'Marry that doctor. He's reliable and respectable. Not like me. And you deserve the best.'

He walked away without giving her a chance to reply and she heard the house door slam as he entered. She didn't follow him at once, knowing that he needed to be alone.

He'd given her a glimpse of the devastation inside his head, even if against his own will. She'd thought she knew the wells of despair and self-disgust that lived there, but now she knew the depths extended further than her worst nightmares. Everything he said was true. If she was wise, she would turn from him to Mr Royce, who could offer her a new life.

But Mark was still the one she wanted; now more than ever. And her resolution was growing. Once before she had lost him by giving in too easily.

She wouldn't let it happen again.

On her way to bed that night, Dee stopped outside Mark's room. Hearing only silence, she opened the door a crack and listened to his deep, even breathing. Finally satisfied, she backed away without a sound.

Inside the room, Mark lay tense until he was certain she'd gone. Only then did he relax, thankful that his breathing had been steady enough to be convincing. After the events of the day, he couldn't have endured having to face her.

He fought to attain sleep. Once it had been so easy. In his untroubled youth he had only to lay his head on the pillow to be in happy dreamland. But that had been—barely five years ago? He was still in his twenties, technically a young man, but, as with so many of his comrades, the inner and outer man no longer matched.

The feeling of being at ease with life had slipped away from him so gradually that he'd barely noticed, until he found himself lying awake at night, which now happened unbearably often. In the hospital he'd been grateful for the sedation that silenced the demons. He could have taken a pill tonight, but he stubbornly refused. He knew Dee checked them every morning to see if he'd had any, and he was damned if he was going to let her know how desperately he wanted to. She already knew too much of his weakness.

At last he felt sleep coming on, retreating, drawing closer, teasing and tormenting, finally invading him, but only to torment him further. Now he was back in the damaged plane... heading back to the airfield...wondering if he'd make it... seeing the ground coming closer...almost there...then the explosion *and the flames!*

He fought to slide back the roof of the cockpit, but it was

stuck. He couldn't get out. He was trapped there while the fire consumed him—trapped in hell. He screamed and screamed but no sound came out. Nobody could hear him—he was abandoned.

'Where are you—where are you—?'

'I'm here, I'm here. Wake up—*wake up!'*

Hands were shaking him, touching his face, offering a way out of the nightmare. He reached for her eagerly, blindly.

'Help me—help me. Where are you?'

Dee saw his eyes open, but vaguely, as though he couldn't see her. He was shivering.

'Mark—Mark, talk to me.' She shook him. 'Are you awake?'

'I don't know,' he whispered. 'The fire—the fire—'

'There's no fire. That was a long time ago.'

'No, it wasn't. It's here; I can feel it—'

'No,' she cried. 'The fire is in the past. It can't hurt you now. I'm going to keep you safe. You're safe *with me.'*

At last, recognition seemed to creep into his eyes. 'Is it you?'

'Yes, it's me. I'm here and I'll always be here.'

She felt him sag in her arms as though the life had gone out of him, replaced by black despair. She tightened her embrace, full of fierce protectiveness.

She'd gone to bed, sad at his rejection of the comfort she had to offer, but, just as she was fading into sleep, the air had been rent by terrifying sounds from the next room. She'd dashed next door to find him sitting up in bed, screaming violently into the darkness. She'd sat beside him, taking him in her arms, but that didn't help. He'd seemed unaware of her, screaming on and on, caught in some terrifying other world where there was only fear and darkness.

She had switched on the bedside lamp, hoping that its light might bring him back to reality, but even when he looked at her she could tell he was still reliving his most ghastly moments, and she was torn by pity and frustration that she couldn't help him except, perhaps, by being there, letting him feel her presence and draw from it what solace he could. If any.

'I'm all right now,' he said bleakly.

Gently, she laid him back on the bed and came closer, propping herself up on one elbow to look down on him.

'Did I wake you?' he asked.

'I heard you being a bit disturbed. It's not the first time but you sounded more troubled tonight than ever before. Were you dreaming about the fire?'

'Not dreaming. Living. It was there all around me and I couldn't escape. I was so scared, I screamed. Isn't that funny?'

'I don't think it's funny at all,' she said tenderly.

'But it is. It's the biggest laugh of all time. I used to think I was so strong. I was a cocky, conceited so-and-so, but I know better now. Just a coward, screaming with fear.'

'You're not a coward,' she said fiercely. 'Any man would have nightmares after what you've been through.'

'I told myself that at first, but they go on and on and I don't know what to do. I'll tell you something that will really make you despise me—' He checked himself.

'Don't say anything you don't want to,' she told him.

'No, you're entitled to know the worst of me. When they said I couldn't go back to the Air Force...I was...I was glad. Do you hear that? I was glad. Oh, I said all the right things about being sorry I couldn't serve my country, but part of me was full of relief.'

'So I should hope,' she said crisply. 'That merely shows you have common sense.'

He stared. 'You're not ashamed of me.'

'No,' she said, almost in tears. 'There's nothing to be ashamed of. Oh, please, Mark, forget all this. You did your bit. You served your country and it nearly killed you. You should be proud, not ashamed. You have a life ahead of you and when you're fully recovered you'll find a way to live it.'

He glanced down at his disfigured chest. 'That will be hard when women can't bear to look at me,' he said.

'That silly girl this afternoon doesn't count. A woman who cared about you wouldn't be troubled by this.'

Suddenly she became aware of a new tension in his manner, and the way his eyes flickered away from her. Looking down, she saw why. She was wearing pyjamas, and in her agitation she'd forgotten to check that the front was properly buttoned up. It had fallen open, revealing her naked breasts.

He was still averting his gaze. She took a quick decision.

'Perhaps it's *you* that can't bear to look at *me,*' she said. 'Am I so ugly?'

'You know better than that.'

'But I don't,' she said softly. 'How could I know?'

Slowly, he turned his gaze back to linger over her breasts, shadowed by the soft lamplight. Then he lay without moving and for a horrible moment she wondered if he was shocked by her forwardness, but at last he reached up to her.

At the soft touch of his fingertips on her breast she felt a blazing excitement go through her, unlike anything she had ever known before. It was the merest whispering caress, but it brought her to life in a way she'd never dreamed of. She heard a long gasp and only dimly realised that it came from herself.

She didn't know how or where the pyjama jacket went, but suddenly he was touching her with both hands, taking her to another world where all the virtuous precepts of her rearing vanished without trace, and there was only this man and her desire for him.

Now all the textbooks were useless. Only her instincts could guide her, and they told her that he was coming to life, pulling away the rest of her pyjamas, then his own, infused with some feeling that made him forget caution, reticence, fear—forget everything except that he wanted and needed her.

For just one second reality seemed to pierce his dream, making him tense as he became conscious again of his scarred chest. Her answer was to lay her lips tenderly against it. She doubted if he could feel the gesture as his burns would have destroyed the nerves, but he would see it, and know that she was glad to reach out to him. When she looked up at his face again, she saw in it a look of wonder.

Then he was pressing her gently back on the bed, moving over her, parting her legs. She gasped at the moment of his entry, clutching him to her, silently saying that the infusion of new life was for him and only him. The moment when they became one was staggering, alarming, like being carried in a roller coaster, higher and higher, up to the heavens, until the devastating peak, and then the giddying descent, holding on to him for safety.

But there was no safety in this new world. There would never be safety again as long as she lived. And with all her soul she rejoiced at it.

She looked up at him, her chest heaving with pleasure, but, to her surprise and disappointment, he seemed troubled.

'I'm sorry,' he groaned.

'But why? Why should you be sorry?'

'It was your first time, wasn't it? Oh, Lord, what have I done? I didn't mean to…I never thought…'

'Neither did I,' she said. 'And I'm glad I never thought. Thought has no place here. Mark, I'm happy. I wanted this. Don't spoil it.'

'Do you mean that?' he asked cautiously.

She gave a smile full of delicious memory. 'Yes, I mean it. Oh, yes, I mean it.'

'Dee, I—' He stopped, choking. Words had always come easily to him, but that was for trivialities, jokes, chatter. Now he longed to tell her of his fear that his skills as a lover had died in the fire and his passionate gratitude to her for helping him rediscover them, and he was suddenly dumbfounded.

'Tell me,' she said.

'It's nothing—nothing—as long as you're all right.'

'Yes, I'm all right,' she assured him seriously. 'I'm more than all right.'

'You weren't just—being a good nurse?'

'Oh, Mark, stop it! You're talking nonsense. As though I would.'

He managed a pale smile. 'I don't know. You take such good care of me, better than anyone else has ever done, ever, in all my life.' He said the last words with an air of wondrous discovery.

'Just the same, there are lengths even a good nurse won't go,' she assured him. Her physical sensations had come swiftly down to earth, but her emotions were still up there, dazed with the joy of being in his arms, feeling at one with him.

Perhaps he felt the same for he suddenly grinned. There was happiness in his smile, but also relief.

Suddenly, Dee chuckled. 'You'll have to marry me now,' she teased.

At once his smile faded and he shook his head. 'Oh, no, I can't do that. I couldn't do you such harm.'

'Harm?'

'Look, I understand that you were only joking, but we both know that I'd be a useless husband. Bottom of the class. The last resort. I only have a job now because of your father's charity, and you'd have to nurse me for ever. I'd be a burden on you, and I can't do that. Just don't make jokes like that any more. All right?'

'All right,' she said with a little sigh that he didn't hear. 'Now, perhaps I'd better go back to my room. The patient has had too much excitement for one night.'

She scrambled back into her pyjamas and was gone without giving him the chance to say anything. After that, there was nothing to do but dive into her bed, hide as far as possible under the covers and curse her own clumsiness.

Why on earth did you have to say that about getting married? What happened to your common sense?

At last she pushed the clothes aside and sat up, eyes blazing into the darkness as she came to a decision.

This was no time for common sense! She had loved him hopelessly for five years, and it was now or never. And if it meant being a 'bad girl', so what? Hadn't her own mother shown the way?

In the corridor outside, Joe stood tentatively glancing back and forth between the doors of Mark's bedroom and Dee's, both of which he'd heard open and close. He hesitated, as though uncertain what a good father would do at this point. When it finally became clear to him, he crept back into his own room and quietly closed the door.

Dee was late home the next evening, to find Mark at the bus stop.

'Have you been there long?' she asked. 'You shouldn't. It's bad for you to stand about.'

'Joe and I were concerned, even after you called to say you had extra duty. He's got the kettle on.'

'Mmm,' she said blissfully, taking the arm he offered. 'How lovely to be pampered!'

'You can't always be the one doing the looking after,' he observed.

'I'm not complaining,' she assured him.

At home, she ate the egg Joe had boiled for her while they all discussed their day. Then they listened to the radio together. In some ways the news was heartening. The Allies had gone on to the attack, taking the airborne fight to the enemy and beginning to land forces in the occupied countries. But this carried a terrible cost.

'How many aircraft have they lost?' Joe murmured sympathetically.

'Over a thousand,' Dee sighed.

Mark cocked an eyebrow at her. 'Did Mr Royce tell you that?'

'I hear things from the patients.'

'Ah, yes, of course.' Mark said no more but his mood became a little glum.

Soon after that, she went to bed and lay listening. She heard the two men climbing the stairs, saying goodnight, going their different ways. After a while she heard Joe cross the landing to the bathroom, then the clank of pipes as he turned on the taps for a quick wash and finally the return to his room. A few minutes later the sounds were repeated with Mark.

Timing was everything. She waited until he'd left the bathroom and was just passing her door before going, 'Ow!'

'Dee?' His voice came through the door.

'Ooh!' she moaned.

'I'm coming in,' he said, opening the door.

She was sitting on the bed, clutching an ankle which rested on her knee. 'I twisted it,' she said feebly.

'How?'

'I couldn't say,' she told him truthfully. 'Rub it for me,' she said weakly. 'That's it! Ah, that's lovely.'

Something in her voice made Mark look at her more closely and see what she'd always meant him to see, that her jacket was open again and her nakedness was a blazing reminder of what they had briefly shared.

'Dee—'

But it was too late. She let herself fall back on the bed so that the edges of material fell apart, exposing all the beauty he'd been trying not to think of since the night before.

'Stop wasting time,' she said, laughing up at him.

Nothing could have stopped him then. When her arms opened in welcome, he went into them like a man coming home, seeking something outside all his previous experience, something he could never have described in words, but which only she could give.

This time she had some idea what to expect and was ready for him, or thought she was. But he still surprised her, taking her to new heights while he looked into her eyes in a way that was new and wonderful, and which made her heart soar.

Afterwards, he didn't draw away so quickly but lingered as though more certain of his welcome.

'What are you thinking?' he asked.

Dee had been wondering how she'd lived so many years without discovering this particular pleasure, but she judged it not the right moment to say so.

'I've been thinking how nice it is to have my Mad Bruin back,' she said. 'Just as mad as ever.'

'Madder,' he assured her. 'Much madder.'

She opened the drawer by the bed and took out the toy.

'You hear that?' she asked sternly. 'You're much madder. He says so, and he ought to know.' She held the little bear to her ear, then said to Mark, 'He wants to know what happened to his friend.'

'I'm afraid I don't know. Things got very confused.'

'Of course,' she said quickly. 'And I suppose you could hardly keep her at the base in case anyone saw her.'

'Right.'

Dee sensed Mark had become suddenly uneasy and made haste to yawn significantly.

'You're tired, I'll go,' he said and hurried away, pausing only long enough to drop a quick peck on her cheek.

When he'd gone, she gave herself a lecture about how foolish it would be to be disappointed. She was no romantic girl, but a warrior converging on her prey. Tonight had gone well. He'd come to her bed and done exactly as she wished. What more was there to want?

A good deal, she thought, *but it'll have to wait. Patience is the quality of great commanders, and I'm going to be the greatest of them all.*

That thought made her feel so optimistic that she fell asleep at once.

One night she came home to find the house quiet. Mark was in the back room, kneeling on the floor, holding Billy in his arms.

'Thank goodness you're here,' he said, his voice cracking in relief. 'Billy's going. The vet came this afternoon and he wanted to put him to sleep, but Joe and I said not until you came home.'

One look told Dee that she'd arrived just in time. Billy was lying patiently, eyes half open, but alert when she appeared, as though he, too, had been waiting for her. Mark handed him gently to her and retreated a little way, staying just close enough to keep a hand on Billy's fur.

'Goodbye, darling,' she choked, holding his head and looking into the old eyes as they faded. 'Thank you for everything. I love you so much—I'll always love you.'

As though he'd been hanging on only to hear that, Billy's eyes closed and his breathing faded to nothing as he fell asleep for the last time.

'Billy,' Dee pleaded. 'Billy, please—just one more minute.'

But he was heavy in her arms and there was nothing to do but lay him quietly on the floor while sobs shook her and Mark took gentle hold of her.

'We were lucky he lived so long,' he said huskily. 'Remember how he nearly hurled himself under my bike?'

'Yes, but for you swerving we'd have lost him long ago. Oh, Billy, Billy!'

Mark held her close, resting his head against hers. She could feel him trembling and for a moment she wondered if he, too, was weeping, having loved the old dog so much. Then he seemed to have a coughing fit and turned hurriedly away.

'Thank you for waiting for me,' she said brokenly. 'I couldn't have borne not to say goodbye to him.'

'Neither could I. Joe said his goodbye before he went out to training, then Billy and I had an hour together. I kept promising him you'd be home in time, but I was becoming afraid you wouldn't. I'm so glad.'

He drew her closer still, for now she was weeping without restraint.

'I'm sorry, I don't mean to—'

'Cry all you want,' he said gently. 'He earned it, didn't he?'

'Yes, he did. He was my best friend. I'm going to miss him so much.'

'You've got me. Of course, I know I'm no substitute for Billy—'

That made her smile, even through her tears. It felt so good to be here with Mark, taking comfort from his kindness, feeling close in a way that was rare. Their shared passion had brought them close but in a different way, one that lacked the sweet contentment that pervaded her now. If only it could always be like this. If only she didn't have to tell him something that would change everything, either for better or for worse. But not yet. For the moment, she would treasure the feeling of being at one with him.

The sound of the clock striking made them draw apart, surprised at how much time had passed.

'I'll take Billy outside,' he said, 'and we'll bury him tomorrow, when it's light.'

He carried the dog out to the shed. As they returned, he said, 'The house is going to be very quiet without him charging around.'

'Not as quiet as all that,' she murmured. 'Mark, I've got something to tell you.'

'Yes? What?'

Absorbed in her thoughts, she missed the hint of eagerness in his voice.

'Well…after the way we've spent the last few weeks…how often we've been together in your room or mine…'

'Dee, will you please come to the point?' he asked tensely.

'I'm pregnant.'

She waited for shock, dismay, she wasn't sure what, but all she saw in his face was frowning concentration.

'It's very soon,' he said. 'How can you be sure?'

'Most women couldn't, but I'm a nurse, so—'

'Of course, you'd know. Dee, I'm sorry.'

'Sorry?' she faltered.

'I took advantage of your kindness. I should have behaved better, but…well, it's done now and…'

'And what?' she asked, almost fearful.

'You once joked that we'd have to get married. How do you feel about it now?'

'Mark, for pity's sake! Is that a proposal?'

'I suppose it had better be. If you think you can stand being married to a bad character. I warn you, I'm no catch.'

'Well, I've always known that,' she said, exasperated almost beyond endurance. 'I'll just have to put up with you, won't I?'

'It's a deal.'

Then there was a pause, during which neither of them knew what to say.

'I can hear Joe coming home.' Mark sounded relieved. 'We'd better go and tell him.'

'Yes, let's.'

That was their betrothal.

CHAPTER TWELVE

THEY married a month later in the church where the others were buried. Joe, bursting with pride and triumph, gave the bride away, and afterwards Dee laid her bouquet of buttercups on her mother's grave.

A few of Mark's comrades from the Air Force were guests at the tiny reception held at home. These days, there were constant air offensives, taking the battle to the enemy, and hope for victory was daily growing.

Dee fell into conversation with Harry, a pleasant man who'd been a good friend of Mark's and was his best man today.

'Dashed if I ever thought Mark would find a woman who could tolerate him,' he confided, laughing.

'I come from a family whose women are renowned for being long-suffering,' she assured him in the same tone.

'Good for you! I say, look at that.' He pointed to a small toy high on a shelf. It was the Mad Bruin, brought out to enjoy the occasion.

'Mark won it for me at a funfair,' she said.

'It's very like his, except that his had a frilly skirt.'

'You've seen his?' she asked, startled.

'I used to. Not recently of course, because it went down with his plane.'

'Mark took it with him when he flew into battle?' she asked, scarcely able to breathe.

'Yes, but don't tell him I told you that. He smuggled it in

secret and none of us were supposed to know, but I think it was his good luck charm, and it really did seem as though he had a charmed life. But in the end they got him, too.'

Someone called him and he turned away, leaving her free to think. Now she was a mass of confusion. Mark had treasured her gift so much that he'd taken it with him while he'd risked his life, and had continued to do so even after she'd broken their engagement. That knowledge caused a glow of happiness to go through her.

But he'd concealed it from her. So many times he could have told her; when they became engaged, when they were making love. Yet he'd chosen not to, showing that there was still a distance between them. Emotionally, he still hadn't turned to her as much as she'd hoped.

And had their encounters really been love-making? On her side, yes, but on his? Hadn't he yielded to desire because he needed to know whether his skills as a lover had survived? And hadn't he married her because, although not exactly what he wanted, it was the best option now available in a devastated life?

But surely she'd always known this? She, too, was settling for what she could get because anything was better than life without him. She would be his wife and the mother of his children. He would never be romantically 'in love' with her. It was too late for that. But his affection would deepen and they would grow close.

She must simply hope for that.

But she refused to be discouraged. She had once promised to love him to the end, no matter what happened, and it was time to keep that promise.

She was taking a risk but it was one she had to take, otherwise her vow of love was meaningless. True love meant keeping on even when the actual emotion was hard to feel.

'Hey, where are you? Dee?'

It was Mark, looking unbelievably handsome, just as she'd once dreamed he would look on their wedding day.

'What's the idea of wandering off alone?' he chided. 'They're ready for the speeches.'

'I'm coming.'

'You're all right, aren't you?' He looked worriedly into her face.

'Yes, I'm fine,' she said brightly.

'Not sorry you married me?'

'Of course not.'

'No regrets? Sure about that?'

She touched his face. 'I'll never regret marrying you, as long as I live. Now, let's go and join the others.'

The rest of the reception went splendidly. There were toasts and speeches, cheers and laughter. That night they made love gently, then lay contentedly together. It was a happiness she'd once thought she would never know.

But she had dreamed of how, on their wedding night, she could finally tell him that she was deeply, passionately, romantically in love with him. Now she knew that she couldn't do it. She would have to wait longer for the right moment. It might be years in coming. Or it might never come.

His pride in his approaching fatherhood was immense. He was home every evening, something that made her an object of envy among her friends, and his whole attitude towards his wife, and marriage generally, exuded contentment. Dee knew that she was lucky, and that it was sheer perversity that made her long for some sign that she was more to him than just the mother of his baby, that he'd married her for more than the refuge she offered.

At last it was time for her to leave her job. On the last day there was a small party in the early evening, with speeches from Sister, Matron and even Mr Royce, who'd found the time to drop in. While he was toasting her, Dee looked up to see Mark standing in the door, a glowering expression on his face that she'd never seen before.

Now she recalled how he'd said that Mr Royce was in love with her, even advised her to catch him and make a 'good' marriage. But that was nonsense, wasn't it? Surely Mark had abandoned that fantasy?

But his scowling face said otherwise.

'I see that your husband has come to collect you,' Mr Royce said genially. 'Take her home, sir, and take the best possible care of her, because she means the world to all of us.'

Mark's smile seemed fixed on by rivets. 'I don't need to be told to take care of my wife,' he said in a soft voice that only Dee and Mr Royce could hear. 'Are you ready to go?'

'Yes, quite ready.'

He drove her home in the battered second-hand car that he'd bought to celebrate her pregnancy.

'You should go to bed now,' he said as they entered the house.

'I'd like some supper first.'

'All right, but then you go to bed. You need all the rest you can get.'

'Excuse me, are you instructing me in a medical matter?' she asked indignantly.

'This isn't medical, it's husband and wife,' he said illogically.

Joe was out that evening, which was just as well, she thought, considering Mark's temper.

'You're not still making a fuss about Mr Royce, surely?' she demanded, annoyed in her turn, and perfectly ready to have a row if that was what he wanted.

'Shouldn't I be? Do you really think he's over you?'

'I'm not sure there was ever anything for him to get over. It was just in your imagination.'

'Like hell it was! Do you think I've forgotten that he's the man you ought to have married?'

'Who says?'

'We both know it's true.'

'Then why didn't I marry him?'

'Because I forced you to marry me.'

Astonishment held her silent. After a moment he turned to see her properly.

'We both know it's true,' he said. 'Once I'd made you pregnant you didn't have a choice. That's what I was counting on.'

'You were…counting…?' She was groping for answers, trying to come to terms with this.

'Why do you think I came to you night after night—?' he growled.

'Or I came to you.'

'I was trying to make you pregnant, so that I could marry you.'

It took a moment for the full glorious truth of this to burst on her.

'You wanted to—you actually wanted to marry me?'

'Don't pretend you didn't know.'

'I've never known. Why didn't you just propose?'

'Because I had no right. What kind of prospect was I? Nothing to offer you beyond a damaged body and a load of nightmares. I didn't have the nerve to ask. But if you were pregnant it would be my duty to marry you, and I could square it with my conscience that way.'

Dee listened to this with mounting disbelief.

'Don't glare at me,' he said. 'Are you angry?'

'Angry? Mark, have you *never* understood? I wanted to marry you, and you were determined not to ask me, so I became pregnant on purpose.'

'What?'

'I had to do it, to force your hand.'

'Do you mean that you…that while I was trying to force… that all the time you were…is that what you're saying?'

'Yes,' she said through twitching lips. 'That's exactly what I'm saying. At least, I think it is. Oh, darling, it's crazy. We each wanted to get married, and we forced each other. And all this time—'

The last words were almost drowned by his shout of laughter. 'Come here,' he cried. 'Come here.'

Crowing with delight, she threw herself into his arms, kissing his face madly, fumbling for his buttons.

'Let's go upstairs,' she urged. 'We have to celebrate this in the proper way.'

But the words acted like a douche of cold water on him, making him freeze in mid-gesture and step back from her.

'What am I doing?' he groaned. 'I must be out of my mind to even think of…I'm sorry—forgive me.'

'Darling, it's all right. We can go ahead.'

'You're pregnant. It could harm you—or our baby.'

'Trust me to know about that. There's a little time left before we have to stop, I promise you.'

She thought she'd swayed him. He reached for her with desperate hands, then snatched them back, groaning.

'No, you're just indulging me, but I won't risk your health. Stay away. Don't tempt me.'

He ran, and a few moments later she heard him in the garage.

She wanted to scream her frustration to the heavens. They had taken one more step along the road, potentially a happy step. He wanted her. He'd wanted to marry her.

True, he hadn't actually said he loved her, but that would come, surely, the first time she could tempt him back into her arms? But he'd made it clear that the baby meant more to him than she did, so for the moment she would have to be patient again.

But she was so tired of being patient.

* * *

After her busy life, it was pleasant to have time for herself and to be cared for by two concerned men. In the afternoons she began putting her feet up, regarding her growing bump with placid contentment.

She was half dozing like this one day when there was a knock on the door. Opening it, she found Harry, the airman who'd been a guest at the wedding.

'I'm afraid Mark's not here,' she told him. 'He's working on a car at the owner's home.'

'It doesn't matter. I just wanted to deliver this.' He held out a large envelope. 'It seems that all Mark's things weren't cleared out when he left and they found this recently. Very sorry. Can't stop, I'm in a hurry.'

He blew her a friendly kiss and departed.

The envelope wasn't sealed and she tipped the contents out onto the table. There were a couple of stray socks and a few papers concerned with his time in the service. It was while sorting through these that she came across the letter he'd written her and never sent:

> …You were right to break it off. I'm a useless character and I'd be no good for you…

The touch of humility took her breath away. He'd spoken like that once before, after his injury, but this had been written before. Had he felt like this even back then? Surely in those days he'd been different, more at ease behind the mask of bonhomie?

From the garage came the sound of clanking as Joe worked away. Mark would be back soon. Gathering everything together, she hurried up to her room and shut the door. Safely alone, she resumed reading the letter.

> …Do you still have the Mad Bruin?…let him remind you of me sometimes; even if it's only the annoying

things…never seem to understand when you want to be left alone…

But I never wanted you to leave me alone, she thought sadly. I wanted more of you, not less.

The letter became disjointed, suggesting that he'd returned to it often, while never finishing it.

Dee threw herself back on the bed, trying to come to terms with the discovery. Her heart was touched by the man she found here, a vulnerable man, not the cockily self-confident loudmouth he tried to present to the world. But someone who was secretly waiting for love to let him down—as it always had done, going back to his earliest days.

This was the true Mark, the lovable Mark, but still the one he concealed from her. The letter had never been sent. She closed her eyes, conjuring him up in the darkness, trying to see him as he must have looked when he was writing. Had he murmured her name?

'Dee—Dee—'

She opened her eyes to find him sitting on the bed beside her, frowning in concern.

'I was just dozing,' she said, looking up at him from the pillow. She saw him looking at the letter in her hand. 'Harry brought some of your things that weren't returned before, and this was among them.'

'So that's what happened to it. So many things vanished, including my little bear.'

'Harry said you had her in the cockpit with you when you went down. He told me that at the wedding. I wish you'd told me yourself.'

He took the letter and she watched his face. He looked sad and strangely older than only a few hours ago.

'Perhaps I shouldn't have read it,' she said. 'You never wanted me to see it, did you?'

'Not then. I didn't know how to face you. There was so

much I wanted to say but I couldn't find the words.' He gave a wry smile. 'I was angry. You dumped me and it was a shock. My pride was hurt. This—' he indicated the letter '—was me trying to say so and making a mess of it. It's probably just as well I didn't send it to you.'

'Or maybe it's a pity. Who knows what might have happened? I might have come to visit you.' There was just a hint of hope in her voice.

'Or you could have had an attack of common sense and stayed well clear of me.'

'Does that mean you're sorry we're together, Mark?'

He frowned, as though not understanding the question. 'How can you say that?' he asked, laying a hand on her stomach. 'Everything that's worthwhile in my life, in the whole world, is here. All hope is here, all love is here, all life.'

He laid his face against her for a moment, then raised it and said gently, 'I'll make you a cup of tea.'

He hurried away, taking the letter with him and leaving her smiling. There was joy to be found in his words, his all-embracing acceptance of her as the hope of his life. She tried to ignore a faint niggling disappointment that his affection seemed to lack the other dimension that would have meant so much. He'd turned to her as a refuge from horrors, something she knew was common to many men who'd been involved in fighting. It was more than she might have expected and if it wasn't what she'd hoped for, so what? With the years stretching out ahead of them, it was time to be realistic.

Wasn't it?

Gradually the war news became more hopeful. Mark was still in touch with many of his pilot friends, and they passed on information not yet available to the rest of the world. In September 1943, allied troops had landed in southern Italy. In January 1944, more troops reached Italy in what became known as the Anzio landings. Their progress was slowed down by fierce resistance, but they overcame it. Hope was in the air.

Then came February, when a few days became known as 'Big Week' as the allied air forces stormed across Europe. The three of them listened to the nightly radio bulletins and Dee tried to read Mark's face, wondering if he felt excluded from what was turning into a triumph. But the smile he turned on her was always warm and tender, and his hand would reach out to touch her stomach gently.

Both Joe and Mark watched Dee like guard dogs. If there was a job to be done away from home it was always Joe who took it, and even he announced that he would soon refuse them.

'This is the last one until it's all over,' he announced one morning, buttoning up his jacket.

'Dad,' she protested, laughing, 'nothing's going to happen for a few weeks.'

'And I'm going to be here when it does. 'Bye darling. Take care.'

She settled down for a pleasant day's sewing, but within an hour she knew she'd been wrong about nothing happening. Pain started tearing through her, growing greater and greater. She screamed and Mark came hurrying in from the garage.

All the way to the hospital she tried to stay hopeful. Her moment was coming. A few hours of suffering and she would see Mark hold their child in his arms, their eyes would meet in a moment of perfect understanding and the bond between them would be sealed as never before.

But, as they reached the hospital and she was wheeled away, she knew that something was badly wrong. The pain was agonising in the wrong way; blood was flowing out of her body in a terrifying river.

'He's dead,' she whispered. 'My baby is dead.'

'We're giving you a blood transfusion,' the sister said. 'Don't give up hope yet.'

But Dee was a nurse. She knew the truth.

'No,' she moaned. 'Oh, dear God, *no!*'

Mark had married her for this baby, hoping to find a haven for his tormented heart. Now she was letting him down.

'No,' she whispered. 'No—please, save my baby.'

Then everything was dark.

For Mark, waiting in a corridor, time dragged with painful slowness. At last a middle-aged nurse emerged, sympathetic when she saw him.

'It's gone wrong, hasn't it?' he asked in a shaking voice. He wasn't sure how he knew, but he'd picked something up from Dee's tension, without understanding it.

'I'm afraid the baby was born dead,' the nurse said.

He closed his eyes, leaning back against the wall, his heart aching for his wife. She was suffering so much, with nothing to show for it.

'But she's going to be all right, isn't she?' he asked huskily.

In the silence that followed he felt terror rise in him. *'She's going to be all right!'* he almost shouted.

'Mr Sellon, I have to be honest with you. Your wife has lost a lot of blood. We're doing our best, but things may not go well. I think you should be prepared.'

'No!' he said fiercely. 'That's not going to happen. I won't let it. You don't understand. She won't go away—because she never does—when I need her—she's always there—' He was breathing hard, as though he'd been running. 'I want to see her.'

'Of course.' The nurse stood back to let him pass.

At first he couldn't believe that the woman lying on the bed was Dee. His Dee was always full of life and vitality, but this woman lay as still as death, her breathing coming so faintly that it was almost noiseless.

'Darling, wake up,' he said urgently. 'Look at me, talk to me.'

There was no response, no sound, no movement, and that frightened him more than anything. In all the time they had known each other, never had she refused him anything, save the time when she'd broken their engagement. And that had been the greatest misfortune of his life. Now she was refusing him again, and the spectre of the future made him recoil in dread.

'You've got to listen,' he said urgently. 'I know you can hear me because—' He stopped as he heard himself saying words he didn't understand. How did he know this? And yet he did know. Somewhere, far back in his mind, he could hear a voice saying, 'I know you're asleep but maybe you can hear me, somewhere deep inside you... I do hope so because there's so much I want you to understand.'

Once he'd heard those words and they had summoned him back from a dark place. Now they were his only hope.

'Can you hear me?' he asked, echoing the words in his memory. 'Can my voice reach deep inside you? Please hear me. There's so much I want you to understand.

'I've never told you of my love because I didn't know how, but I must tell you now because it may be my last chance. I think I loved you from the start. Remember how easily we could talk? That's why I couldn't commit to Sylvia. She was beautiful but you had something special about you, although I didn't properly understand.

'I was a young idiot, full of self-importance, thinking I was entitled to everything I wanted, especially girls. And all the time this feeling was growing in me but I couldn't let myself admit the truth. It mattered too much. *You* mattered.

'I was glad when we decided to pretend to be a couple because I wanted you to be my girl. So why didn't I ask you? Because I was shy, and that's the truth. There, laugh at me. I deserve it. I was a fool. If I hadn't been, I'd never have lost you. I went out on the town to convince myself that I was still in charge, free of you, when the truth was I could never be free. And you threw my stupidity back in my face, as you had every right to do.'

Mark laid his head down on Dee's breast. 'Speak to me,' he begged. 'Come back to me. I love you with all my heart. I'll never love anyone else.'

As he spoke, a door opened inside his mind and he knew that these words, too, were not his own, but had been said to him, long ago. He hadn't recognised her love until this moment, but it was as true now as then, deeper with the depth of suffering, and his own love reached out in response.

Everything that mattered to him had come from the woman who lay in his arms, who would slip away if he couldn't prevent it. He did the only thing that was in his power, laying his lips on hers, sending her a silent message of warmth and love.

'Can you feel my love reaching out to you?' he murmured, repeating what he now knew to be her words to him long ago. 'It's yours if you want it.'

For a long moment he held his breath, letting it out slowly as her eyes opened.

'It was you, wasn't it?' he whispered. 'You came to me in the hospital when I was dying, and you turned me back. Now I'm here to do the same for you.'

'Is it true?' she murmured. 'Is it really true?'

'It's true, my darling, more true than I can ever say. You're the one, the only one. You always have been. Do you remember how you ordered me to get well, saying you were a bully? Well, so am I.' He gave a shaky smile. 'Woman, your husband is ordering you to get well and love him for ever.'

'Then I must,' she said.

'Is that a promise?'

'It's a promise.'

'I'll hold you to it.'

Suddenly her smile was stronger. 'Did I ever break a promise to you yet?'

He shook his head and spoke sombrely. 'I love you, my wife. It took me too long to say it, but now I'll be saying it every moment of all the years ahead. I love you. I love you.'

The months that followed were a mixture of grief and joy— grief for our dead child, joy that we had found each other at last. Everything was sweet and familiar, my darling, yet everything was new.

You became a little more possessive, always checking to see that I was all right. People used to say to me, 'Doesn't he suffocate you? Isn't it annoying?' But it wasn't annoying. It was lovely being needed.

I remember 6th June which became known as D-Day, the start of the Normandy landings, when the allied army invaded the Continent again, this time in France. Now the final victory was in view. The war didn't end officially until the following year but D-Day was the beginning of the end, and people sensed it, pouring into the streets to sing and hold hands, looking to the future with glad hearts.

We were there, too, standing with our arms about each other, trying to rejoice with the others. I was determined to put a brave face on it for your sake, but when I glanced up I found you looking down at me with an expression of such love and concern that I felt closer to you than ever before. That night my happiness had nothing to do with the looming end of the war. It came from knowing that I came first with you.

For a while we feared that I couldn't have another baby, and I'll never forget how tenderly you assured me that you didn't care about that, as long as you had me. But then we found I was pregnant again, and before long we had Lilian. The following year Terry joined us. You wouldn't admit how proud you were to have a son. People were just beginning to talk about women's lib and you didn't want to appear old-fashioned. So you tried to seem casual, but I knew you were bursting with pride and I had a little laugh—secretly, of course.

But no happiness is ever untroubled. The following year Polly was born and it seemed we could ask for no more. She was your favourite. According to Dad, it was because she looked like me. When she died suddenly, just before her first birthday, I thought you, too, would die. I believe you wanted to, although you never said so. We didn't talk about it, just held each other in silence, night after night.

Your health improved. You got much of your strength back and Dad made you a partner in the garage. As he got older he eased off a bit, doing less mechanical work and helping to look after the children so that I was able to go back to work at the hospital. You didn't like my working. In those days a wife and mother was supposed to stay at home, but you said I must do whatever I thought right.

I think it helped that Mr Royce had got married to a beautiful girl twenty years his junior.

Once I'd started work you never mentioned it, never complained, even helped in the house to make my life easier. People who'd known you before the war were astonished. 'You should have seen him back then,' they'd say. 'You'd never have thought he'd turn out like this.'

If you had a fault it was that you were always losing things. How many times did I hear you cry, 'Dee, where's my—?' Heavens, but you were the untidiest man in the world! Still are, come to that.

For a while there were five of us in that little house and it was very crowded, but we were happy, and when Dad died we really missed him. We watched our children grow up and make their own lives, and then we were alone for the first time.

Some parents are devastated when their young fly the nest, but you said it was like being newlyweds. We were in our fifties by then, but you were right.

What a time we had! We got quite exhausted. We thought of having a honeymoon, because we hadn't had one the first time, but in the end we just locked the doors and had a honeymoon at home.

Then, in a strange way, we became parents again. Lilian gave birth to Pippa just when she was getting ready to go back to work, and she was glad when we offered to help out. We cared for Pippa part-time until she started school. And when she was a teenager we took her in because she and Lilian couldn't live in the same house without squabbling. And now it's a joy to have her here, our extra 'daughter', caring for us and understanding us better than anyone else.

I told her about having our 'honeymoon' at home, and she was scandalised. She thinks it's not a honeymoon unless you go away and we should have taken that trip to Brighton that we once talked about. Perhaps she's right. Is it too late? We've done everything else, could we still manage that, too? Oh, yes, let's do it. Let's have one last wonderful fling!

'Are you crazy?' Lilian demanded.

'No, they're crazy,' Pippa laughed. 'And why shouldn't they be?'

'Brighton? At their age?'

'They won't do anything energetic, just sit in the sun. I'll be there to take care of them, and I'll bring them home safely. Promise.'

A week later she drove Mark and Dee to the seaside resort in a trip that was planned to be as similar as possible to the one they would have taken years before. They stayed in a tiny bed and breakfast near the seafront and spent each day strolling gently along the promenade, or sitting in deckchairs on the beach. At these times Pippa moved away far enough to give them privacy, but always kept them in sight in case they needed her.

'I really envy you two,' she said once, when she'd just

finished making them comfortable. 'The way you are to-gether—it's wonderful.'

'And one day it will be wonderful for you,' Dee promised. 'With the right man.'

'No.' Pippa shook her head. 'Not now. I'm finished with all that.'

'And you're going to spend the rest of your life like this?' Dee demanded. 'Doing dead-end jobs and turning your back on love? I'm not going to let that happen. I've got plans for you, my girl. I've left you some money in my will, but only on condition you train for a proper career. No, don't argue.'

'But Gran, I—'

'Listen my darling; Grandpa and I planned this together. We've had a wonderful marriage and we can't bear to think of you losing out, when we want you to be as complete and fulfilled as we've been. Let us have the peace of knowing that we did our best to help you, and then we'll always be part of your life.'

'You'll always be part of it anyway. You know that.'

'You obey your Gran,' Mark said contentedly. 'I always have.'

'I'll—think about it.'

'You'll do as you're told,' Dee said. 'Be off with you, now.'

'Thank you,' she said softly.

She kissed them both and strolled away to the water's edge, where she could paddle, yet still look up the beach and keep a protective eye on them as they sat in contented silence, eyes closed, faces raised to the sun, their hands entwined, like their hearts. This was how love ought to be.

I don't think it will ever be like that for me, Gran, whatever you say, she thought. *But you're so convinced that you make me think I might be wrong. If, one day, a man comes along who helps me forget the past, maybe it will work out between us, because I'll have my memories of you and Grandpa to remind me to hope and believe. I'll never forget what you and he have taught me, and I thank you both with all my heart.*

Coming Next Month

Available February 8, 2011

BABIES AND BRIDES!

Wedding bells and the pitter-patter of tiny feet
can be heard in Harlequin® Romance this month
as we celebrate bouncing babies and radiant new brides!

#4219 THE NANNY AND THE CEO
Rebecca Winters

#4220 THE BABY SWAP MIRACLE
Caroline Anderson

#4221 PROUD RANCHER, PRECIOUS BUNDLE
Donna Alward

#4222 DAYCARE MOM TO WIFE
Jennie Adams

#4223 EXPECTING ROYAL TWINS!
Melissa McClone

#4224 MILLIONAIRE'S BABY BOMBSHELL
Fiona Harper

REQUEST YOUR FREE BOOKS!
2 FREE NOVELS PLUS 2
FREE GIFTS!

HARLEQUIN® *Romance*®

From the Heart, For the Heart

*Harlequin Romance author Donna Alward is loved
for her gorgeous rancher heroes.*

*Meet Wyatt as he's confronted by both a precious
little pink bundle left on his doorstep and his neighbor Elli
who's going to show him the ropes....*

Introducing
PROUD RANCHER, PRECIOUS BUNDLE

THE SQUAWKING QUIETED as Elli picked the baby up, and
Wyatt turned around, trying hard to ignore the feelings of
inadequacy as Darcy immediately stopped fussing.

"Maybe she's uncomfortable. What do you think, sweet-
heart?" Elli turned her conversation to the baby.

"What do you think is wrong?" Wyatt asked, putting the
coffee pot back on the burner.

A strange look passed over Elli's face, one that looked
like guilt and panic. But it was gone quickly. "I couldn't
say," she replied.

"But you were so good with her this afternoon." Wyatt
put his hands on his hips.

"Lucky, that's all. I just...remembered a few things."
The same strange look flitted over her features once more.

Wyatt took the coffee to the table. "You fooled me. You
looked like you knew exactly what you were doing." So
much so that Wyatt had felt completely inept. A feeling he
despised. He was used to being the one in control.

Elli and Darcy walked the length of the kitchen and
back. After a few moments, she admitted, "I haven't really
cared for a baby before. The things I thought of were simply
things I'd heard about. Not from experience, Mr. Black."

Her chin jutted up, closing the subject but making him

want to ask the questions now pulsing through his mind. But then he remembered the old saying—*Don't look a gift horse in the mouth.* He'd benefit from whatever insight she had and be glad of it.

"I don't really know what babies need," he said. "I fed her, patted her back like you did, walked her to sleep, but every time I put her down…"

Wyatt almost groaned. Of course. He'd forgotten one important thing. He'd been so focused on getting the formula the right temperature that he'd forgotten to check her diaper. Not that he had any clue what to do there either.

Pulling calves and shoveling out stalls was far less intimidating than one tiny newborn.

"She's probably due for a diaper change, isn't she." He tried to sound nonchalant. This was a perfect opportunity. Elli must know how to change a diaper. He could simply watch her so he'd know better for the next time.

Instead, Elli came around the corner of the counter and placed Darcy back in his arms. "Here you go, Uncle Wyatt," she said lightly. "You get diaper duty. I'll fix the coffee. Cream and sugar?"

Oh boy, Wyatt thought, looking down into Darcy's pursed face, his smug plan blown to smithereens. He was in for it now.

Will sparks fly between Elli and Wyatt?

Find out in
PROUD RANCHER, PRECIOUS BUNDLE

Available February 2011 from Harlequin Romance

Try these Healthy and Delicious Spring Rolls!

INGREDIENTS

2 packages rice-paper
spring roll wrappers
(20 wrappers)

1 cup grated carrot

¼ cup bean sprouts

1 cucumber, julienned

1 red bell pepper, without
stem and seeds, julienned

4 green onions
finely chopped—
use only the green part

DIRECTIONS

1. Soak one rice-paper wrapper
   in a large bowl of hot water
   until softened.

2. Place a pinch each of carrots,
   sprouts, cucumber, bell
   pepper and green onion on the
   wrapper toward the bottom
   third of the rice paper.

3. Fold ends in and roll tightly
   to enclose filling.

4. Repeat with remaining
   wrappers. Chill before
   serving.

Find this and many more delectable recipes
including the perfect dipping sauce in

USA TODAY bestselling author

Sharon Kendrick

introduces

HIS MAJESTY'S CHILD

The king's baby of shame!

King Casimiro harbors a secret—no one in the kingdom
of Zaffirinthos knows that a devastating accident has left
his memory clouded in darkness. And Casimiro himself
cannot answer why Melissa Maguire, an enigmatic English
rose, stirs such feelings in him…. Questioning his ability
to rule, Casimiro decides he will renounce the throne.
But Melissa has news she knows will rock the palace
to its core—*Casimiro has an heir!*

Law dictates Casimiro cannot abdicate, so he must find a
way to reacquaint himself with Melissa—his new queen!

Available from Harlequin Presents
February 2011

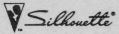

ROMANTIC
SUSPENSE

Sparked by Danger, Fueled by Passion.

NEW YORK TIMES BESTSELLING AUTHOR

RACHEL LEE
No Ordinary Hero

Strange noises...a woman's mysterious disappearance
and a killer on the loose who's too close for comfort.

With no where else to turn, Delia Carmody looks
to her aloof neighbour to help, only to discover
that Mike Windwalker is no ordinary hero.

Available in February.
Wherever books are sold.

Visit Silhouette Books at www.eHarlequin.com

SRS27709R2